daisy drama club

STAGE FRIGHT!

written and illustrated by
belinda roberts

BEETLEHEART
PUBLISHING
www.beetleheart.co.uk

Daisy Drama Club - Stage Fright!
was first published
in the United Kingdom in 2012
by Beetleheart Publishing.

Whilst this work is inspired by the original Daisy Drama Club
all characters appearing in this work are fictitious.
Any resemblance to real persons, living or dead, is purely coincidental.

ISBN
0-9540208-6-3
978-0-9540208-6-6

Daisy Drama Club - Stage Fright! © 2012 Belinda Roberts
The moral right of the author has been asserted.

Illustrations © 2012 Belinda Roberts

Contents

To all the members
of the original

daisy drama club

How It All Began

Sophie and Cressida loved acting. They were best of very best friends and were simply bursting to be in a play. Imagine the crazy costumes! The stage make-up! The characters they could play: a trapped princess, a wicked stepmother, perhaps a hairy lion or a little frightened mouse! Imagine waiting backstage! The first night! The audience cheering!

BUT Sophie and Cressida had a big, big problem. They were very lucky in one way. They lived in the agreeable village of Wissop which had a pretty playground, the sweetest of sweet shops, a babbling brook, splendid trees to climb and lots of other perfectly good and useful things for children to enjoy BUT *no* drama groups or acting classes or theatre companies whatsoever! Even worse than that, when ancient aunts or school teachers or plain nosy people asked Sophie and Cressida what they would like to be when they grew up they would both say 'an actress' and all these well meaning grown ups would say,

'oooh lovely!',

'wonderful!',

'how simply SPLENDID!'

But it really wasn't any good wanting to *be* an actress if they never *did* any acting!

One absolutely boiling hot August day towards the end of the long summer holidays Cressida came round to play with Sophie. Nearly every day Cressie was at Sophie's house or Sophie was at Cressie's. Some things were different about the girls. Sophie was tall-ish, Cressie was small-ish, Sophie had long-ish hair, Cressie had short-ish hair, Cressida thought of good ideas and worked them out whilst Sophie thought of good ideas and leapt on them. Both girls were afraid of sharks but that is not important in this story. Some things were the same about the girls (apart from liking acting, of course). They wore similar clothes, their favourite sweets were Fizzy-Pops which fizzed like mad in your mouth then suddenly went pop and always surprised you even though you KNEW the pop was coming, and, most importantly, they thought the same things as only best friends do. Today they played their favourite game of acting out their made up play *The Gobbling Goose and The Ferocious Fox*.

'Squawk! Squawk!' screeched Sophie.

'Snap! Snap!' yelled Cressie.

But it was swelteringly hot and the girls were so, so fed up of *pretending* to act and not *really* acting. Puffed out, they flopped down on the grass amongst the daises and gazed up at the sky.

'If only we could be in a proper play!' said Cressie for the hundredth, millionth time.

Sophie was too hot to answer. The friends lay in silence for a few minutes watching two small, white clouds drifting across the endless blue above them.

'The main problem,' said Cressida at last, with a sigh, 'is even when we pretend to do a play it's so difficult only having two people.'

The girls fell into silence again, and started idly picking daisies. Cressida, who always liked to be doing something useful, started making a daisy chain.

'And it's hard to even practise acting and drama with only two people,' added Sophie after a while. She closed her eyes, feeling sleepy.

Cressie added another daisy to her chain. She stared at what she had just made and she got that special feeling you often get when you are just about to have a VERY GOOD IDEA. One or two daisies alone can't do much, she thought, but join a few together and ...

'Look Sophie! A daisy chain!'

Sophie opened her eyes and squinted.

'Lovely Cress.'

'Not just lovely. This daisy chain has given me an idea. We could ask some friends to come round and do some drama with us!'

Cressie held up the daisy chain. Sophie caught Cressie's excitement and sat up too and took hold of the other end of the chain. The two girls stared at each other thinking exactly what each other was thinking in only the way a best friend can.

'I know!' they said together. 'Let's start a drama club!'

'What shall we call it?'

The daisy chain dangled between them.

'I know!' they said together again, '*the Daisy Drama Club*!'

And that was the beginning of the

... or DDC as it came to be known.

Putting up Posters

September came and the Michaelmas term at Wissop Village School started. On the first morning the playground was full of children chatting excitedly about the holiday just finished and the term ahead. But Sophie and Cressida had only one topic of conversation – their new Daisy Drama Club! They were soon busy telling everyone about their brilliant idea – but it was not as easy to get people to join as they thought it would be. Bonnie Brackett said she was far too busy with her swimming lessons. Tara 'tippy-toes' Williams said she would like to come but couldn't because she had to concentrate on her ballet. Elsa who was in the class above Sophie and Cressida said it sounded like a silly idea. Elsa's best friend, Rosalie, who always agreed with Elsa, said the last thing she wanted to do on a Saturday morning was to mess about learning lines.

Despite feeling a bit disappointed the two girls spent the rest of playtime making posters which they planned to put up in school and around the village.

After school they asked Mr Gumtree at the village shop if they could put up a poster in his shop window.

'Of course! Delighted to help! You will be inundated by young thespians! Oh what a joy! What

GUMTREE STORES

a thrill! Always wanted to tread the stage myself but the lure of the village shop called and here I am … and I am quite content! Quite happy! You see, to me, *this* is my stage!'

'This?' queried Sophie looking around at the chaotic piles of tins, cereal packets, baskets of fruit, bunches of flowers and endless jars of sweets.

'Yes! This counter is my stage! My produce are my props! Customers are my audience! Every time the door opens and the shop bell tinkles I get that prickly feeling up the back of my neck. Nerves! Stage fright!

But then I deliver the immortal words 'Good afternoon madam! How can I help?' and my performance begins and my confidence grows. When a purchase is made, to me that is the applause!'

'Wow!' said Cressida impressed. 'I never knew running a village shop could be so thrilling.'

'Nor did I!' added Sophie. 'Thanks Mr Gumtree. Come on Cress, we had better put up our posters.'

'Best of luck girls,' said Mr Gumtree from behind his counter and Sophie was sure that he actually gave a slight bow before turning away to stack some more tins of butter beans.

'What shall we do if hundreds of people want to join?' asked Cressida anxiously as they fixed their poster up between one for ' 'Woof! Woof' Dog Training' and another for 'Fab Floristry for All'.

'Just the first ten to arrive can join. The rest will have to go on the waiting list,' said Sophie. 'But with Elsa spreading such horrid rumours about the club I don't think we need worry about too many people!'

A Royal Arrival

The Daisy Drama Club would take place on Saturday mornings at Sophie's home, The Old Farmhouse. At nine o'clock on the day the club was to open Cressida was already at Sophie's making last minute plans. Suddenly there was a loud banging sound. Sophie looked out of her bedroom window.

'It's Uncle Max!' she shouted and ran outside.

Uncle Max had driven into the yard in his old yellow banger which was pulling a wobbly trailer, stacked high with sticks of wood, precariously piled up and tied on with an old fraying rope.

'Hello chaps!' he bellowed at Sophie, as his car came to an abrupt halt. 'Is this where the Royal Shakespeare Company performs?'

Uncle Max was big and hairy. He had an enormous beard that hid the lower part of his face, huge, thick rimmed glasses that hid the middle part of his face and massive tufts of hair sticking out all over the place, springing out from the top of his head that hid the rest of his face. Sophie had no idea what he really looked like but he was jolly and fun and more than that, always full of surprises!

'Uncle Max! It's not exactly the Royal Shakespeare Company. Not yet anyway. What have you got in your trailer?'

'That jumble is actually a load of mini sized chairs for you and your fellow actors and actresses. Jolly good bit of kit. Need a few nails here and there. Then they'll be as strong as anything.'

'Tip top! Thanks Uncle Max!' said Sophie jumping up and down. 'Let's get them into my bedroom quick Cress and put them in a circle ready for when everyone arrives.'

But Cressie was staring in amazement at somebody grinning at her from Uncle Max's back seat.

'Ah Cressida!' Uncle Max chortled. 'That's King Arthur! I thought you might like to welcome him as the royal patron of your theatre company. Come on out, Your Highness!'

Uncle Max swung open the back door of his car and hauled out a life-sized model of King Arthur, splendid in a deep red velvet cloak and golden crown. He leant the monarch against his car and bowed.

'Your Majesty, I present to you Miss Sophie and Miss Cressida, both loyal subjects devoted to the world of theatre.'

'Wow, Uncle Max!' cried Sophie.

'Weird!' said Cress, not sure if she meant King Arthur or Sophie's Uncle Max.

'Weird but wonderful! That is the essence of theatre!' said Uncle Max, who had spent many happy hours on stage. 'But let us not delay! Onwards and upwards - chairs into action!'

The three carried the chairs and King Arthur up to Sophie's bedroom where the first meeting was to be held. Sophie's room was only just big enough to hold eight chairs in a circle. King Arthur was put in a corner where he looked regal and imposing.

Uncle Max produced a hammer and paper bag of nails from inside his roomy jacket and set about mending chair legs and backs. After each chair had been attended to Sophie or Cress in turn had to sit down and test it out. Uncle Max gave it a shake from the back and declared each chair 'as safe as houses' or that it would 'last a lifetime that fellow!'

When he had finished he gave a final bow to King Arthur and departed.

Downstairs the doorbell rang.

'Visitors!' called up Sophie's mum, who had been surprised to see royalty and chairs carried upstairs. Sophie rushed downstairs. How many children would be there, waiting excitedly to join the DDC?

The First Member

Sophie opened the door and there stood the formidable Mrs Theodora Whistle-White. Tucked down besides her, almost hidden in her mother's furry white coat, was her daughter ... frail little Susannah-Sue Whistle-White. Susannah-Sue Whistle-White had very pale skin, fluffy, mousy coloured hair and in Sophie's opinion was very feeble and MUCH too young to join the DDC. There was nobody else.

'Go on, darling,' hissed Mrs Whistle-White prodding Susannah-Sue. 'I've come to join the Daithy Dwama Cwub,' Susannah-Sue said shyly. Or at least that was what Sophie thought she had said. But Susannah-Sue had spoken so quietly that it was impossible to tell.

'Susannah-Sue absolutely adores drama,' gushed Mrs Whistle-White.

'You're going to be an actress when you grow up aren't you Susannah-Sue, darling. So naturally talented. Destined for stardom. She auditioned for a new TV drama. She would have got the part if the director hadn't been so blind. Couldn't spot star talent when there it was right in front of his nose. Silly, wretched little man. Anyway that hasn't stopped you Susannah-Sue, has it darling.'

Susannah-Sue just shook her fluffy head and looked bewildered.

'Where is everybody anyway?' went on Mrs Whistle-White, Sophie thought, rather rudely.

'Upstairs,' said Sophie quickly. 'Come with me Susannah-Sue and meet the others.'

'Bye darling!' Mrs Whistle-White gave Susannah-Sue a peck on the cheek leaving a bright pink lipstick mark and added in a low voice to Sophie, 'Susannah-Sue is very, very talented Sophie. You're extremely lucky that she's got time to join your club with all her other commitments. Just remember, my precious daughter is a star in the making. She will be excellent in the lead role in your plays. Farewell for now!'

Sophie was furious! What a rude mother!

And why had she brought Susannah-Sue?

Did she think the DDC was some kind of nursery for babies?

Sophie stomped upstairs and into her bedroom with Susannah-Sue trailing behind her. Cressida, who had been putting handwritten notices about the DDC out on the chairs, looked surprised when she saw the little girl with Sophie - and nobody else!

'Where is everyone Sophie? Hello Susannah-Sue. Are you lost?'

'Not lost. She's come to join the DDC,' interjected Sophie.

Cressida was surprised but had practised what she was going to say to new members so thought she might as well test it out on Susannah-Sue.

'Welcome to the Daisy Drama Club, Susannah-Sue. First of all, do you have any infectious diseases?'

Cressida had a great and grim aunt who had returned from the exotic tropics with a horrid disease that made her neck grow excessively long and her nails turn into viciously sharp talons. The disease was very infectious so Cressie knew all about the dangers of this sort of thing and that, like the great and grim aunt, they were best avoided. Susannah-Sue did not understand the question so Cressie hoped for the best and went on.

'We hope you will be very happy and learn lots about drama and dance and acting. Now would you like to fill out one of our membership forms?'

daisy drama club
MEMBERSHIP form

Do you have any infectious diseases?
☐ YES ☐ No

Name . . . .

How old are you? . . . . . .

Can you learn lines ?
☐ Yes   ☐ No

Who is your favourite
character? . . . .

What is your favourite
food? . . . . . .

Other important things
about you?

PLEASE DRAW A PICTURE
OF YOURSELF HERE

Jumping jellybeans! Sophie was impressed. Cressida had saved the situation. Only one member who was too young to *be* a member was an absolutely, catastrophically disastrous start to the club. But at least one member was a teeny weeny bit better than no members. They had better get going.

After half an hour they had gone through warm up exercises that Cressida had found in a book on drama and were reading their way through a short play called *The Revenge of the Raspberry Bun*. It was going exceedingly badly. Susannah-Sue was having difficulty in reading her lines so they had to keep stopping to help her. She also spoke *so* quietly that even if she *was* speaking they could hardly hear what she was saying. Sophie became exasperated.

'Speak UP!' she said to Susannah-Sue.

Tears sprung to Susannah-Sue's eyes.

'You're mean and howwible!' she cried, for the first time in a loud voice. 'I don't even want to be in your thilly cwub but my mamma *made* me come. I want to go home! I want to go home! I want to go home!

TAKE ME HOME!

TAKE ME HOME!

TAKE ME HOME!

WAAAAAAAAAH!'

Sophie and Cressida could not believe how wide Susannah-Sue could open her mouth! They stared at her in amazement. The crying got louder and louder until she reached a tremendous, continuous howl. She stopped momentarily to take a big gulp of breath and in that moment the doorbell rang.

'More visitors,' called up Sophie's mum.

'Oh no!' said Sophie as Susannah-Sue started howling at top volume again. 'Be quiet Susannah-Sue! I'm sorry! I didn't been to be horrid! Please, please stop crying!'

'I'll look after her,' shouted Cressida with her fingers in her ears. 'You go down and find out who's here. It might be more members!'

'That's what's worrying me,' said Sophie. 'If they hear all this noise they'll never want to join!'

Sophie went downstairs and opened the door.

There were Harriet and Henrietta the twins, otherwise known as Harry and Hen. They were lively girls with bright red hair, big smiles, freckles and massive front teeth.

'Hi!' said Harriet grinning. 'We've come to join the club. That's if you've got any spaces left.'

'Leaping liquorice! What's all that noise?' asked Hen. 'Sounds like someone crying! Is it someone from the club?'

''Fraid so,' said Sophie embarrassed.

'Leaping liquorice times two!' said the twins impressed. 'That's good. Sounds really realistic! Can we join?'

'Yes! Great! Of course you can,' said Sophie. 'Come on up.'

Sophie led the way up to her bedroom dreading to see the twins' reaction when they realised it really *was* someone crying. But when she opened the door there was Susannah-Sue sitting next to Cressida, a big smile on both their faces. Sophie was astonished.

How had Cressida managed to cheer up Susannah-Sue so quickly?

Even more impressed, Sophie watched her best friend welcome the twins.

'Welcome to the Daisy Drama Club, Harry and Hen. Do you have any infectious diseases?'

'Just freckles,' said Harry.

'And goofy teeth,' added Hen.

'We can accept freckles and goofy teeth,' said Cressida. 'Welcome to the DDC. We hope you will learn lots about drama and dance and acting. Would you like to fill out one of our membership forms? Oh and meet our other member Susie White and King Arthur our royal patron.'

'I thought it was Susannah-Sue Whistle-White,' whispered Sophie to Cressida.

'It is. But she hates that silly name and put Susie White on her membership form. That's what she wants to be called. I said fine and she was as pleased as punch. It certainly stopped her crying!'

'Good for you Cressie!' said Sophie grinning.

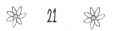

Once the twins had got over their surprise at meeting King Arthur and finished chatting with Susie they filled in their forms. Then followed a much better read through of *The Revenge of the Raspberry Bun* with the twins taking part with great gusto, and even Susie speaking up a little so that Sophie felt a tiny ray of hope that the club could be a success after all.

Ten minutes before the end Sophie disappeared, returning with a tray of drinks and two and a half biscuits.

'Sorry this was all we had,' she apologised. But two and a half biscuits were much better than no biscuits so the five members of the DDC shared them out and chatted excitedly about plans for the glittering future of the Daisy Drama Club.

A Spooky Idea

News spread around the village about the DDC. The next Saturday two more members joined: Beaky West and Lou Lightman. Sophie's mouth dropped wide open when she saw Lou at the door. Lou was Elsa's younger sister and Elsa had been spreading pretty mean rumours about the DDC all week.

'May I join?' asked Lou awkwardly. 'I know Elsa is being horrid about the club but I think it's a brilliant idea.'

'Of course you can join,' said Sophie admiringly. After all it had been pretty brave of Lou to come along. It must be awful to have a sister like Elsa!

Upstairs Cressida welcomed the new members, gave them a membership form and introduced them to King Arthur. They had done their warm up exercises and were just acting out the second act of *The Revenge of the Raspberry Bun* when there was a tremendous commotion outside. A dog was barking, a pony neighing and the sound of a girl shouting, 'Pickle! Pickle! Stand still. Take your hoof out of that flower pot! Oh stop nibbling the pansies!'

Then there was a loud knock on the door. Sophie ran downstairs and there was Abby Bagwash, Farmer Bagwash's daughter with Lollipop the sheepdog and Pickle her very shaggy, cheeky pony.

'Sorry I'm late,' said Abby breathlessly, 'but Pickle let himself out of his field and I've been looking for him everywhere.

In the end I found him poking his head through the window of Gumtree Stores trying to steal an apple! Sorry but here I am at last! Pickle *stop* eating the flowers! Could I join the DDC?'

Abby was red in the face, her hair had bits of straw sticking out of it and her T-shirt was on inside out.

Sophie could not stop laughing, until Pickle stood on her toe.

'Ow!'

'Pickle get off you naughty boy! Sorry Sophie. I expect you don't want someone with such a pickle of a pony in your club!'

'It's a drama club, not a pony club! Of course you can join!'

'Terrific! Can I tie Pickle up to your gate? Lollipop, you guard Pickle and make sure he doesn't get up to mischief. Behave yourself Pickle.'

Abby gave the mischievous pony a severe look and a loving pat then followed Sophie upstairs.

'Hi everyone!' said Abby giving a general wave to the DDC. 'Here at last! Oh! Who's that wriggling about?'

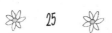

She reached in her top pocket and pulled out a small white mouse.

'Bertie! What are *you* doing here? Sorry everyone! Bertie stay in my pocket, keep still and *no* squeaking!'

Abby stuffed Bertie back into her pocket and grinned round at the DDC. Harry and Hen were giggling but little Susie was sitting rigid in horror, her eyes transfixed on Abby's pocket!

Towards the end of the meeting Harry and Hen, who always liked action, asked when they were going to actually perform a play.

'Christmas!' said Sophie quick as a flash. Cressida looked surprised. Christmas! That was only three months away. But she realised it was important that the members thought that she and Sophie knew what they were doing so she added, 'Yes Christmas!'

'What play are we going to do?' asked Beaky, whose real name was Sarah, but everyone called her Beaky because the had the longest, sharpest nose you have ever seen. She kept her nose in a book - which means she was always reading - not that she took her nose off and left it in a book - and it was rumoured she kept it extra sharp so she could turn pages with it so she could read super fast. Beaky was used to the name now and didn't mind. She was actually rather proud of her nose and thought of it as a friend. Beaky was also practical and liked to know the facts.

'Something Christmassy I hope,' said Lou. 'Lots of holly and ivy and carol singers and mistletoe and snow and oooh I love everything Christmassy!'

'Will we have to sing carols?' asked Abby appalled. 'I'm a terrible singer. Dreadful. Everyone sticks their fingers in their ears when I start. Pickle can neigh more tunefully than I can sing!'

'It's going to be...' said Sophie pausing and looking at Cressida for help.

'... *A Christmas Carol,*' finished off Cressida.

CHARLES DICKENS

'The one with Scrooge and all the ghosts?' said Beaky her eyes wide with delight. 'I read that last Christmas. It's really spooky!'

'Oooooh!' cried Harry and Hen together, waving their arms and rolling their eyes.

'That's it!' said Sophie. '*A Christmas Carol.* Charles Dickens wrote it didn't he Cress?'

'Definitely,' said Cress with authority.

'I don't really know that thory,' said Susie shyly. 'Could you tell it to me?'

'I know the story,' beamed Beaky. 'Shall *I* tell it to you?'

'Yeth pleath.'

Beaky looked round and seemed to be pointing at everyone with her sharp nose, checking everyone was listening. 'I'll see how much I can remember...'

Beaky pointed her nose in the air, tapped it a couple of times as she often did when she was thinking, closed her eyes and started.

A CHRISTMAS CAROL AS TOLD BY BEAKY

Once upon a time, a long time ago, at least a hundred and fifty years ago, that's Victorian times of course, there lived a very mean man called Scrooge who was mean as mean can be and he earned heaps of money but kept it all for himself and he didn't spend it, oh no, he just liked piling it up and piling it up and piling it up and his friend who worked with him was Jacob Marley and he was just as bad but Jacob Marley died and Scrooge carried on working and making even more money and piling it up even higher and in his office he had an assistant called Bob Cratchit who was a clerk, which means he had to write down lists and lists of numbers using a big feather quill pen which I would like to try one day and Bob Cratchit had a wife and lots of children and they tried to be happy but they were very, very poor but even being poor they could have been happy because they were a happy family if you see what I mean but they had one big, heavy heartbreaking sadness that hung around their house like great

※ 29 ※

clouds of sad dust which was that their youngest son, called Tiny Tim, who was tiny, had something wrong with his legs and had to walk with a crutch, hobble, hobble, hobble, hobble which made them sad and even though Scrooge had lots of money he hardly paid Bob Cratchit anything and didn't bother to help Tiny Tim not one bit.'

Beaky paused and opened her eyes. She checked everyone was still listening, put her nose in the air again, tapped it twice, closed her eyes and continued.

'One Christmas Eve Scrooge went home and had the fright of his life because Jacob Marley, who was dead, appeared to him as a ghost on his door knocker. Chains rattled! Bells rang! Door knockers knocked! Scrooge was terrified because Marley was covered in heavy, heavy chains, each chain a punishment for each sin of his life and he had lots of those but even though he had lots he was warning Scrooge. 'Beware Scrooge!' - that is Marley speaking, not me. 'Your chain is much, much longer than mine and much, much heavier because you have led an even worse life than me but you are lucky Scrooge because you are being warned and tonight three ghosts will visit you who are the Spirit of Christmas Past, the Spirit of Christmas Present and the really scarey one the Spirit of Christmas Future. which made Scrooge shiver and shake with fear but he got into bed and then the spirits came one by one. Ooooooh! Oooooh! Ooooooh!'

Beaky, with her eyes still closed started waving her arms about and swaying. She seemed to be going into some sort of trance.

'Ooooooh! Ooooooh! Ooooooh! The spirits showed Scrooge how wicked he had been but saddest of all the Spirit of Christmas Future showed Scrooge what was going to happen to poor, poor Tiny Tim!'

Everyone stared at Beaky. Her voice had gone all crackly. She had opened her eyes and was staring into the distance. A large tear was dripping off the end of her nose.

'Doth Tiny Tim die?' whispered Susie.
But Beaky did not hear.

'Then the most terrifying moment of all comes when Scrooge falls into his own grave.

aaaaaaaaaaaaaaah!'

Beaky fell to the ground and lay stone still.
No-one said a word.
Suddenly Beaky leapt to her feet and danced around the room.

'Church bells ring! Carol singers sing! It's Christmas Day and Scrooge wakes up a completely different man all jolly and so excited he kisses and hugs everyone!'

Beaky ran round kissing and hugging everyone.

'He goes round to the Cratchit family and gives them the most enormous turkey and lots of presents and promises to pay for Tiny Tim to get better.

Beaky ran round pretending to give out presents. Then she sat down and with eyes glowing she tapped her nose and said,

'and that's the end of the story.'

'Tho it doth have a happy ending.'

'Yes. In the end.'

'Leaping liquorice. Sounds great!' said Harry.

'Leaping liquorice. Brill!' said Hen. 'Super spooky!'

'Wait,' cried Beaky suddenly, looking serious. 'I've just had a terrible thought. It's a book not a play!'

'You're right,' answered Cressida. 'Just one thing for it. We'll have to turn it *into* a play. We need someone to write a script.'

Sophie looked surprised. Cressie was good at thinking fast!

'Please, please could *I* do that?' said Beaky, finding it hard to breath with excitement. Beaky's dream was to be a writer.

'Beaky, you would be the perfect script writer!'

Beaky beamed and tapped her nose.

'Leave it to me!'

'But *where* are we going to perform the play?' asked Abby. Sophie's room was already squashed with eight children and King Arthur.

'Not in here!' said Sophie.

33

'What about the barn?' suggested Cress.

Many years ago Sophie's house used to be part of a farm. The farmhouse itself was on the road going through the village with its land stretching out behind. By the time her parents had bought the house most of the land and farm buildings had been sold off. But one barn remained which was right next to the farmhouse. At the moment it was filled with wood and lots of junk. But, thought Sophie, Cress was right. It could make the most wonderful theatre!

'Great idea Cress! Let's go and have a look.'

The eight trooped downstairs and out to the barn.

The barn was a large, pale yellow stone building with a slate roof. There was a huge entrance held up by an ancient timber. Inside were more great black beams and you could see right up to the roof of one half. Swallows swooped out in fright when they saw the children. The floor above was covered in floorboards to half way along and reached by an old wooden staircase. Sophie led the way, climbing over boxes and planks. She climbed up to the floor above and poked her head through the square gap in the floorboards where the staircase peeped through. It was gloomy and dusty. She sneezed before going on. At last standing on the first floor she realised that because the floor only covered half of the floor below you could look down onto the ground floor.

'The stage could be down there and up here could be the lighting gallery,' said Sophie excited. 'We could have lights up here and shine them down onto the stage below. The audience could sit on seats down there. The perfect theatre!'

'Perfect!' said Cressie.

By now all the members were up on the first floor.

'What's through that prehistoric door?' asked Beaky, pointing with her nose.

At the far end of the first floor was an ancient oak door hung on mighty black hinges.

'That,' said Sophie in a hushed whisper, 'is The Forbidden Door!'

'The Forbidden Door?'

'What do you mean?'

'Where does it go?'

'I mean that it goes nowhere. Open that door and you step out into fresh air. There's a huge drop to the ground below, so dad said we must *never* open it because if we did we might fall into nothingness. That's why we call it The Forbidden Door.'

'It was probably used for throwing out hay bales in the olden days,' said Abby, getting Bertie out of her pocket to give him a look around. 'Look Bertie! If you escape you must *never* go near The Forbidden Door. You might have a nasty fall!'

Bertie squeaked in alarm and Abby put him safely back in her pocket.

Beaky turned their attention to more practical matters. 'It's very dusty and dirty,' she said, sniffing. 'We'd have to clear everything out. Where would we put all the stuff?'

That was a problem. Just then they heard a shout.

'Sophie! Is that you? What *are* you doing? It's dangerous up there! Come down at once!'

It was Sophie's dad.

Sophie's dad was lots of fun but he was also pretty strict. Sophie knew she was in trouble!

'I'm coming down dad,' she called back, leading the way down.

Sophie's dad could not believe his eyes. Out of the barn came not only Sophie, but also seven other little girls, all now blinking in the bright sunlight and all covered in dust and dirt.

'Sophie! What on earth are you up to? I thought you were running a drama club not an explorers' club!'

'I'm sorry dad. It's just that we need somewhere to perform our first play. We're going to do *A Christmas Carol* and we thought the barn could be a good theatre.'

Somehow it sounded a bit silly saying this to her dad.

'A theatre? The old barn! Really Sophie, sometimes I think ...' His voice trailed off as he strode over to look inside the barn.

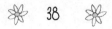

'Hmmm! Well I have been thinking of getting all this junk cleared out,' he said.

'Do you mean that we might actually be able to use it as a theatre?' said Sophie, her eyes opening wide in astonishment.

'No! I did not say *anything* about turning it into a theatre. But you have made me think about getting it cleared up. Once we've got rid of the junk we'll see how safe it is. Now you better all get cleaned up otherwise you'll be called the Dusty Drama Club!'

Sophie and Cressida grinned at each other. It was just possible that they might be on the way to having their very own theatre!

Disaster for Cressida

The good thing about Sophie's mum and dad was that once they got keen on something they got super keen!

'Right,' said dad when he came back from work on Monday, 'let's get going!'

'Going where?' asked John in surprise, looking up from his drawing of yellow-winged darter dragonfly. John was Sophie's younger brother and was as crazy about insects as Sophie and Cress were about acting.

'Barn clearing and theatre making,' said dad. 'Chop chop! Put on your old clothes and lets start moving all that junk!'

Just then Cressida turned up.

Sophie could immediately see that something had happened - and probably something bad!

'We're going to clear out the barn and make the theatre Cressie! Come upstairs and I'll lend you some old clothes.'

As they rummaged through Sophie's cupboard looking for old T-shirts Sophie asked Cressida what was the matter.

Cressida forgot about the T-shirts, sat down on Sophie's bed and told Sophie the dreadful news.

'It's worse news than the worse news you could even begin to imagine. We're moving! We can't afford the rent any more at Hawthorne Cottage so we've got to move out before Christmas. There's nowhere else to rent in Wissop so we're moving to Ditch!'

'Moving to Ditch!'

Sophie was shocked. Cressida was the very best sort of best friend you could possibly have. She could not imagine not having her practically next door. And what about all their plans for the DDC?

'Oh Cressie! That is the worst news ever! Worse than ... but are you sure? Couldn't you ask if you could stay on a bit longer?'

'No. We've had the cottage for ten years but the rent has gone up and dad can't afford to pay. Our landlord, Farmer Bagwash, wants the cottage back to give to someone who can pay the right price for it.'

'Farmer Bagwash! But that's Abby's dad. Do you think she knows?'

'I don't know. Anyway the fact is we've got to go.'

'Couldn't you buy somewhere in Wissop? Somewhere really cheap?'

'Mum and Dad have looked but the houses are too expensive. You don't earn that much money painting and decorating.'

Cressida's father, Tim was a painter and decorator and her mum, Polly, was brilliant at the piano and gave lessons in between looking after Cressida and her three brothers and sisters. Even so, there was never much money left over.

'Come on girls! What's all that chattering? We've work to do out in the barn!' Sophie's dad called up to them from downstairs.

'Cheer up Cress!' said Sophie. 'Ditch isn't that far away. Perhaps something will happen like we find a pot of gold in the barn and you won't have to move after all.'

Cressida smiled. Sophie was good at cheering her up. As she went out of the room she caught sight of

King Arthur and started. Could she have seen correctly? Did he just *wink* at her? Perhaps things were going to work out for the best after all... but she couldn't imagine how!

By the end of the week they had cleared all the junk out of the barn. Every evening when dad got home he put on his old clothes and got to work. He piled up the ancient timber in a great stack at the end of the yard, took eight sacks of rubbish down to the skip, sold off an old lawn mower and gave away boxes and boxes of books to a local charity shop. Mum got 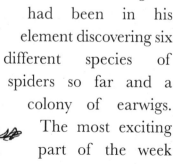 busy sweeping out the dust and whitewashing the walls. It was starting to look much better!

Sophie, John and Cressida helped, managing to get covered in cobwebs, dust, dirt and whitewash. John had been in his element discovering six different species of spiders so far and a colony of earwigs. The most exciting part of the week had come when John and Cressida pulled off an old sheet covering a great stack of junk that had been hidden away at the back of the barn.

'More chairs!' shouted Cressida in glee. 'Look! Lots and lots of chairs!'

'What's so exciting about *more* chairs?' asked John.

'What do audiences sit on? Chairs of course! There must be thirty here. Perfect!'

'Perfect!' said Sophie, dropping her paintbrush and running across to see what all the commotion was about. 'These old wooden stacking chairs will be perfect for the grown ups and the little ones can sit on the chairs Uncle Max gave us!'

At that very moment, right on cue, there was a hooting sound. In drove Uncle Max in his old banger pulling his faithful trailer. In the trailer were four large objects covered in sacking.

'Hello chaps! I've got a cracking surprise for you!' he said jumping out of the car. He went to the trailer and dramatically pulled back the sacking.

There lay four big, black metal objects.

'What do you think of those beauties?' he cried triumphantly.

'Err beautiful,' said Sophie.

'Interesting,' said Cressida.

'What are they?' asked John.

'Lights of course!' said Uncle Max enthusiastically. 'Theatre lights! Stibblewick Theatre is being completely refurbished so I went along to see if there was anything useful they didn't want and they gave me these. Four real stage lights - or lamps as we call them in the theatre industry - and a dimmer pack. Of course, they didn't actually *give* them to me. I had to buy them - but at a bargain price. So if you want them you can buy them off me for the same bargain price.'

'How much?' asked Sophie.

'Ten pounds for each lamp. Forty pounds for the lot including the dimmer pack!'

'Forty pounds!' Cressida was shocked. She knew how hard it was to earn that much money.

'We haven't even got one pound yet!' said Sophie.

'Tell you what,' said Uncle Max, 'let's bang them straight into action. We'll hang them up in the barn right now. Then if you reckon they could help you put on some cracking shows you can borrow them to begin with and once you've raked in a bit of loot from your audiences you can start to buy them off me. Does that sound a tip top scheme?'

'Tip top!' said Sophie grinning.

Inside the barn were great beams stretching across from side to side. It was very easy to hang the lamps over each beam. The barn had electric sockets and with the help of two extension leads dad managed to get them plugged in. They pointed the lamps towards the end where the stage would be.

'What's going to be your first performance?' asked Uncle Max.

'*A Christmas Carol*!' said the girls.

'*A Christmas Carol*? That's the one with that Scrooge chappy isn't it? Hmmm. Lots of ghostly light I reckon,' said Uncle Max thoughtfully. He got out his penknife, and cut some string tied up round the neck of a canvas bag. 'You'll need some spooky green light, and a bit of blood red, this icy blue and perhaps some white,' he added pulling out strange looking plastic coloured sheets.

'Sounds great!' said Sophie not quite sure what Uncle Max was up to.

At the front of each lamp was a metal bracket. Into the bracket Uncle Max slotted a sheet of coloured plastic. 'These are coloured filters called gels,' he explained. 'Slip a gel into this bracket on the lamp like this and it gives you a coloured light. These metal flaps here are called barn doors. They help shape your beam and cut out 'spill' or light that you don't want. See how you can flap them open and shut. The dimmer pack here allows you to alter the power of a lamp. You can make the light brighter or dimmer. I'll show you! Go and get King Arthur.'

Sophie and Cressida were surprised by this request but then Uncle Max was a rather surprising sort of person. They soon came back with King Arthur and Uncle Max sat him on a chair where the stage would be. Outside it was dark.

'Now pretend Arthur is Jacob Marley about to appear to Scrooge as a ghost. Quick! Take your seats for the show!' said Uncle Max.

He switched off the normal lights and waited a few
moments. It was pitch black in the barn. Sophie,
Cressida, John, mum and dad all waited in silence
wondering what was about to happen. Nobody said
a word. Slowly they noticed a very faint green light
shining eerily onto King Arthur's face. It made him
look real and ghostly at the same time. The light got
stronger. Then it became mixed with red and blue
until the whole stage area was bright with colour.
Then the colours all faded away. It was dark again.
Nobody spoke. Somebody started clapping at the
back of the barn. Uncle Max switched on the normal
lights - or house lights as he called them - and there
was Cressida's mum, Polly.

'Bravo,' she said smiling. 'I can see this is going to
be a real theatre!'

'I didn't know you were here,' said Cressida
pleased but surprised to see her mother.

'It was getting dark so I came up to walk you home.
There was no one about at the house and then I saw

this green glow coming from the barn so I thought I better come and have a look. Very impressive too.'

Everyone was grinning in delight. Uncle Max had given them a real glimpse of what could be done.

'It was magical,' said Sophie enthusiastically.

'It'll be brilliant for *A Christmas Carol*, lighting up the ghosts,' added Cressida.

'Well let's hope that you do lots and lots of productions,' added Uncle Max. 'How lucky you children are to have a theatre of your very own. Wissop is a wonderful village!'

Cressida looked sad. 'Come on Cressie,' her mum said. 'We'd better be going home.'

'See you tomorrow Cressie,' called Sophie. She felt so sorry for her friend. If only she didn't have to move. And now they'd got another problem. How on earth would they raise forty pounds for the lamps?

Rehearsals Begin

The next Saturday was an important date for the DDC. Sophie and Cressida had decided that meetings should take place in the barn from now on. They carried all the little chairs down from Sophie's room, across the yard and into The Barn Theatre as it was to be called and arranged them in a circle. All the members arrived at ten o'clock prompt, except for Abby. They were just about to start when there was the sound of a pony trotting quickly up the road.

'Now you stay there Pickle and be good. Pickle don't look at me in that cheeky way and don't untie yourself from the gate.'

There was the sound of patting and a neigh and Abby burst into the barn.

'Sorry I'm late everyone! I was just grooming Pickle when he somehow untied himself and trotted off. Every time I got close to catching him he trotted off a bit further. Anyone would think he was playing a game!'

Abby sat down hot and flustered.

'Oh my goodness! What have you done to the barn. It looks flippin' fantastic!'

Everyone was astonished by all the work that had been done. Not only did they have a building but chairs and lamps! It looked so different from the week before that even the least imaginative member of the DDC could start to believe it could be a theatre.

'You must have worked very hard,' said Beaky.

'Mum and dad helped quite a lot,' said Sophie.

'A lot of a lot!' added Cressida.

Everyone said they'd like to come and help with any more sweeping and cleaning.

'I'll ask my dad if we can borrow his extra big broom we sweep the farmyard with. He's really kind at lending things,' said Abby enthusiastically.

Cressida and Sophie exchanged glances. Did Abby know that because of her father Cressida was going to have to leave the village?

'Why is your father...,' began Sophie but seeing Cressida frown she stopped in her tracks. Perhaps it wasn't right to talk about non-DDC things in the meeting. Instead Sophie suggested they all had a good look round The Barn Theatre and then the meeting could begin in earnest.

'What are we going to do for a stage?' asked Beaky.

Sophie's dad had had an idea for the stage.

'See those old book shelves?' explained Sophie. 'Well, we're going to lie them down on the ground and then dad is going to nail chipboard on top. The only trouble is we've got to buy the chipboard and dad says it'll cost about twenty pounds which the DDC will have to pay for.'

'Pay for!' exclaimed Beaky, tapping her nose. 'But we haven't got any money!'

'No. I know. We've also got to pay for the lights.'

'How much will the lights be?'

'Forty pounds.'

'*Forty pounds!* That's sixty pounds we need already and we haven't got any money at all!' wailed Harry.

'Let's think about this,' said practical Beaky. 'How many people can sit in this theatre?'

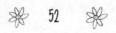

'Forty,' said Cressida 'and more if we squeezed extra people onto benches.'

'Right, if we charge fifty pence a ticket to come and see *A Christmas Carol* we'll make er...'

'Only twenty pounds,' finished off Hen who was wizard at maths.

'We could thell some raffle tickets ath well,' suggested Susie, shyly.

'And programmes,' added Harry.

Suddenly Sophie felt that raising the money was going to be more of a challenge than a problem!

'What wath the thecond important announthement?' asked Susie, a little louder than usual. She was actually starting to enjoy being a member of the DDC!

'The second announcement is THE SCRIPT!' said Cressida excitedly, forgetting all about leaving Wissop and moving to Ditch.

Beaky had been busy. Beaky's grandpa, whose name was Albert and who also had a very sharp, pointed nose and was very deaf, lived in Wissop in one of those terraced cottages that is crammed so full of books that when you open the front door you have to squeeze down a tunnel of bookshelves just to get to the kitchen at the back. When Beaky went round to his house and told him about the DDC and that

they were planning on performing *A Christmas Carol* and did he have a copy she could borrow because she was writing the script, he leapt in the air and waved his walking stick around in delight.

'Oh I am as light as a feather, I am as happy as an angel' he yelled. 'That's a quote you know! Straight from Dickens!'

Albert loved Dickens. *Oliver Twist* had been his very favourite story when he had been a boy and he had all the books Charles Dickens had ever written.

'I have a copy somewhere ... somewhere...' he said at top volume, excitedly.

They searched through piles of books but could not find *A Christmas Carol*. Suddenly Albert held up a dusty copy and shouted 'Dickens! *Oliver Twist*!'

'Grandpa! It's *A Christmas Carol* we are looking for not *Oliver Twist*.'

'Ah, but *one* Dickens novel means we are getting *close*,' said Albert tapping his nose.

The next discovery was *David Copperfield*, then *Nicholas Nickleby* then *Bleak House*, then *Hard Times* ... and just as Beaky thought they would have to give up - *A Christmas Carol*!

'Oh I'm as merry as a schoolboy! Whoop!' yelled Albert, triumphantly. 'That's another quote you know! Straight from Dickens!'

'Let me help you write the script,' said Albert and he dragged out an ancient typewriter. 'You tell me what to type and I will type. What's the first line?'

Beaky stared at the book. Writing the script was going to be much harder than she thought. She tapped her nose.

'I don't know where to start.'

'At the beginning I should think,' said Albert. 'Dickens words are magnificent so let's use them as much as possible, cut down on the number of characters otherwise you'll need a cast of thousands, make it rhyme to make it easier to learn and have lots of bits for the audience to join in. What do you think?'

Beaky hugged her grandpa. What would she do without him!

It was with a great deal of pride that Beaky handed out a copy of the script to each member at the meeting.

'Tiptop!' said Cressida impressed.

'Now we just need to decide the cast. That is who is going to be who?' said Beaky beaming. 'We, that is grandpa and I, have drawn up a list of all the characters in the play.'

'We could audition,' suggested Cressida.

'Oh no!' squeaked Susie in horror.

'We could think who was most like which character.'

'Who is the meanest?'

'Who is the most spooky?'

'Does anyone have a bad leg?'

'Is anyone dead?'

Cressida looked worried. These were not good suggestions.

'With acting,' said Beaky thoughtfully, 'you just need to get *into* the character. You *pretend* what they are like. You don't actually have to *be* mean to *act* mean.'

'You're right Beaky. Let's run through the list and put your hand up if I read out a character that you think you could pretend to be.'

'Tho you don't have to be dead to be a thpirit?'

'No Susie.'

'Or have a bad leg if you want to be Tiny Tim?'

'No Susie.'

CAST LIST

Jacob Marley — Cressida

Scrooge ⎯ Sophie

Spirit of Christmas Past — Hen

Spirit of Christmas Present — Harry

Spirit of Christmas Future — Lou

Bob Cratchit — Beaky

Tiny Tim — Susie

a Miseltoe — Abby
  Spirit

Other parts to be played by everyone — we will sort this out

PROMPT — Beaky

LIGHTING — John

58

'Although, I do have a *bit* of a bad leg. Look I fell over yethterday and got a brewth on my knee. It'th very thore but that would help wouldn't it?'

'Yes Susie.'

By the end of the meeting, after much to-ing and fro-ing, all was agreed. Cressida produced the final, final cast list. Everyone was happy although Susie was still anxious.

'I know I will be able to hobble like Tiny Tim ath I do have a bad leg tho I can pwactith but do I have to thay vewee much?' she asked nervously.

Sophie remembered how she had upset Susie on her first day and was determined not to do so again.

'Not if you don't want to,' she said kindly. 'When you've read the script Beaky can change it if you are still worried.'

'Could I be the prompt as well?' asked Beaky.

'Yes!' said everyone apart from Susie.

'What doth the prompt do?'

'The prompt keeps a copy of the script backstage. If anyone forgets their lines during the play the prompt just reads a few words out to help them get going again,' explained Cressida.

'I bet that will be me!' wailed Susie. 'I'll be thow, thow nervouth!'

'No you won't,' said Cressida, 'because we will

have so many rehearsals. And anyway even if you do forget your lines Beaky will prompt you.'

'Rely on me!' said Beaky tapping her nose. Susie smiled at Beaky gratefully and tapped her own little nose in reply.

'Who is *Mistletoe*?' asked Abby curiously.

'Mistletoe is head of the spirits. It was grandpa's idea. They are Jacob Marley's helpers. They are not actually in the book but he thought it would be fun if we had a spirit chorus. It's a sort of alternative to all the ghosts that are actually flying around in the book,' explained Beaky. 'We've called them Christmassy names like 'Roastchestnut' and 'Plumpud'!'

'Let's try it out!' said Cressida. 'Everyone can be a spirit for now. Look this is how the chorus goes on page six.'

Everyone turned to page six of the script.

'Let's stand in a row and read it out.'

The girls stood in a line and this is what they read:

```
We are spirits, ghosts and ghouls.
We float on your whispers,
     fly on laughs ...
```

'Wait! Wait! Stop! Stop! Stop!' interrupted Sophie horrified. 'That sounds terrible. Absolutely awful!

Dreary and so feeble! We're meant to sound like spirits. Mysterious! Scarey! Spooky! Bwaaahhaaa!'

Cressida was not sure if Sophie was pretending to be a spirit or was upset so she added, 'And it's also got a rhythm. Let's clap to it as we say it, like we do in music lessons at school.'

The DDC tried again.

This time it sounded much better:

```
SPIRITS
We are spirits, ghosts and ghouls.
We float on your whispers, fly on laughs,
Hide in cupboards, bubble in baths.
We rise in bread, sparkle in jewels,
We are spirits, ghosts and ghouls.
Yeah.!


MISTLETOE I put the giggles into tickles.
ROASTCHESTNUT I put the prick
     into prickles.
PLUMPUD I make sound into song.' La! La! La!
SNOWBALL I make you get your
     homework wrong ... Ha! Ha! Ha!
```

SPIRITS
We are spirits, ghosts and ghouls.
We float on your whispers, fly on laughs,
Hide in cupboards, bubble in baths.
We rise in bread, sparkle in jewels,
We are spirits, ghosts and ghouls. Yeah.

ALMONDWHITE I put the tick into the tock.
CANDIEDFRUIT I put the hole in your sock.
CINNAMONSTICK I spin rainbows in the air.
ANGELSPRITE I spin tangles in your hair!

SPIRITS
We are spirits, ghosts and ghouls.
We float on your whispers, fly on laughs,
Hide in cupboards, bubble in baths.
We rise in bread, sparkle in jewels,
We are spirits, ghosts and ghouls. Yeah.

By the end of the meeting they had even worked
out some actions.

'Could everyone try and learn their lines by next
week?' said Cressida.

'Leaping liquorice! Next week!' shrieked Hen.

'Leaping liquorice times two! Next week!'
shrieked Harry.

'I'll never ever, ever, ever learn all those words by then!' wailed Abby, taking out her little mouse. 'Bertie you'll have to help!'

Susie had gone horribly pale and the whites of her eyes showed as she stared in horror at Cressida 'Learn all thwose linthes by next thweek!' she whispered in a tiny, breathy little voice.

'The other thing is costumes,' said Cressida.

'Costumes! Did you say costumes?' said Lou excited.

'Any ideas what we could do for costumes?'

'I think,' said Susie, 'before we can make any cothtumeth we need to know what they *look* like tho why don't we all draw a picture of what we think our own cothtume will look like and bring it with uth to the next rehearthal. It might altho make uth think about our character a bit more.'

'Jumping jellybeans Susie! That is a tiptop idea,' said Sophie.

Susie smiled pleased with herself. Already she was imagining what she would draw for Tiny Tim's outfit.

The meeting came to a close. Everyone left except Sophie and Cressida

'Scripts, costumes, lines to learn ... there's quite a lot to do when you're putting on a play isn't there.'

'Mmmm,' said Cressida. 'What's more,' she added gazing around the barn, 'I suppose most people can just concentrate on the play without having to worry about making a theatre as well!'

Things to DO

The weeks sped past and the DDC members *did* learn all their lines and rehearsed hard on Saturday mornings.

They also made lots of lists.

After one rehearsal Cressida read out one of her now famous 'THINGS TO DO' lists:

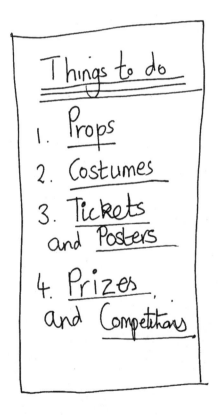

Things to do

1. Props
2. Costumes
3. Tickets and Posters
4. Prizes and Competitions

'I vote that we start making the posters and tickets now,' said Beaky when Cress had finished, 'and then we can chat about the props and costumes and raffle prizes while we're working.'

'Good idea!' said Sophie. 'I'll go and get some paper and crayons.'

They made some very colourful posters and exciting looking tickets. Each member managed to make one poster and five tickets which made eight posters in all and forty tickets.

'Leaping liquorice! Those are brill!' whistled Hen.

'Leaping liquorice! Really pro!' added Harry.

'I think we're getting well organised,' said Beaky, tapping her nose.

'Elsa won't be able to say the club is silly now,' said Lou.

'My dad says it's a really good club,' said Abby 'He likes me coming along. He says it keeps me out of mischief and stops me causing chaos with Pickle round the farm!'

'Do you think your dad...?' began Sophie.

Cressida knew what Sophie was going to say. Luckily Beaky, who had been furiously scribbling some sums on a scrap of paper interrupted.

'I've worked it out! If we sold forty tickets to children at 25p each we would make ten pounds. If we sold forty tickets to adults at 50p each we would make twenty pounds.'

'But that's nowhere near the sixty pounds we owe Uncle Max and your dad, Sophie!'

'We could make some more tickets and people could sit on the benches.'

'We'll make them,' volunteered Harry and Hen.

'We could sell raffle tickets.'

'And have a lucky dip.'

'And sell refreshments at the interval.'

'How about hot dogs?'

'Candyfloss?'

'Popcorn?'

'What about more Christmassy things. Things to do with *A Christmas Carol*?'

'Roast chestnuts?'

'Mince pies?'

'That hot mouldy wine stuff grown ups drink.'

'You mean mulled wine!'

'That smells weird but it does smell of Christmas,' said Cressida writing down the ideas at top speed. 'Lets all make some mince pies - well ask our mums too.'

'We could heat the mulled wine up in the kitchen and bring it straight out to the theatre when people arrive and in the interval,' said Sophie.

'We could have hot chocolate for us children.'

'Leaping liquorice! My favourite!' added Harry.

'And mine!' said Cressida. 'Now what about costumes? Have we got all the drawings at last? Harry and Hen I think yours are the only ones missing now.'

Everyone had kept forgetting to do their drawings or had left them at home at other rehearsals. It was getting closer and closer to the performance and Cress and Sophie were getting worried. Harry and Hen grinned and gave their drawing to Cressida. At last they had them all. Cressida stuck the final sketches into a scrap book she had entitled 'Costume Designs for *A Christmas Carol*'.

'I'm thorry about my paper,' said Susie. 'It was all mamma could find.'

'I'm sorry about my paper too,' said Abby. 'Bertie decided to eat it. Also I'm sorry about my drawing. I could only think of a stick of mistletoe and the stick I've drawn doesn't even look like mistletoe!'

'I hope you wear a bit more than that on the night,' said Beaky peering at Abby's picture.

Harry and Hen giggled.

'I think Lou's is the betht,' ventured Susie. 'Thimple but effective.'

'Thanks Susie!' said Lou, surprised but pleased with the compliment.

'My plethure,' replied Susie.

'I think they are all tiptop,' said Sophie.

'Tip top,' added Cressie. 'But now we've got to turn the drawings into costumes. We need a wardrobe mistress.'

'Could *I* be the wardrobe mistress,' begged Lou. 'I can sew and I'm learning to use a sewing machine. It's really speedy. Brrrrrrrr. We can borrow things like trousers and jackets and I can make the rest. Even a costume for you Abby.'

'Thanks Lou,' said Sophie and Cressie delighted.

'When the costumes are ready we can hang them along this beam so they'll all be here and ready for the performance,' added Sophie.

'Aha! Our wardrobe!' said Lou, her eyes gleaming.

'You better have the costume book,' said Cressida handing a delighted Lou the book of drawings.

The meeting came to a close.

'Let's work hard at putting up posters and trying to sell all the tickets,' said Cress as everyone left. 'We've only got two weeks to go before the show. And don't forget to get going on the mince pies!'

When everyone had gone Sophie walked back with Cress to Hawthorne Cottage. It was a pretty stone cottage, with apple trees in the garden and a vegetable plot where Cressie's dad grew lots of food.

'Are you really going to have to go?' asked Sophie.

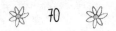

'Worse news than worse news, yes,' replied Cressida. 'We've got to leave on December 13th. Mum and dad have found somewhere in Ditch to rent, so we'll be there before Christmas.'

'Have you asked Farmer Bagwash if you could stay for just a little longer?'

'I'm sure mum and dad have. But he wants the cottage back.'

'There must be something we could do!' said Sophie.

'I don't think so,' said Cressida gravely. 'Bye Sophie.'

'Bye Cress,' said Sophie as her friend opened the garden gate and ran up the path to the cottage door.

Sophie walked home feeling frustrated. What could she do to help Cress? Around the corner she bumped into the mean Elsa Lightman and her nasty friend Rosalie.

'How's your wonderful club going?' sneered Elsa sarcastically. 'I'm afraid my baby sister Lou is so disappointed because nobody in our family will be able to come to your play. We are all be busy doing something else more interesting - not wanting to hurt your feelings or anything. Bye.'

Elsa and Rosalie skipped off giggling. Tears pricked Sophie's eyes but she walked on trying to ignore the horrid girl's remarks. She felt really angry. Without thinking about it she found herself reciting her speech that Scrooge makes in act one when *he* is furiously angry with his nephew for wishing him a *Happy Christmas*!

'Don't be such a crotchety old carbuncle dearest uncle!' says the nephew.

Scrooge replies,

```
What else can I be
When I live in such a world of fools
Who bake their brains with revolting
    Merry Christmas rules?
If I had my way every nitwit
    wishing me a merry season
Would give me bloomin' good reason
To boil them in their own plum pudding
Chop them into mincemeat tart
And bury them with a stake of holly
    through their heart!
```

It was a dramatic speech and made Sophie feel much better. Elsa and Rosalie could be as mean and nasty and spiteful and gruesome as they liked but there was no way Sophie would let them spoil the show!

A Terrible Fright

On Wednesday night after school the girls decided to get together for an extra rehearsal. It was a cold, dark, rainy night and the wind rattled the slates on The Barn Theatre roof. Inside Lou tipped out a bag full of her old toys she had sorted out for the lucky dip.

'Wow!' said Hen.

'Brill!' said Harry.

'I've got some pwizes for the raffle,' said Susie shyly. 'Mamma gave thith bag to me jutht ath I was leaving. I don't know whath in it. Thall we have a look?'

'Yes please!' said Sophie.

Susie tipped the bag upside down. Out fell:

... a gold, shimmering, sequined evening bag ...

... a satin make-up bag embroidered with the words '*My Couchy-Couchy-Sweetheart*' ...

... a purple, fluffy hat made of ostrich feathers ...

... a furry, orange shawl with yellow tassels ...

... a pair of pink stiletto shoes with little yellow butterflies sewn on the points.

Susie went as pink as the shoes in her embarrassment.

'Wow ...' said Hen, uncertainly.

'Brill ...' said Harry, even more uncertainly.

'Perhaps,' said Lou tactfully, 'some of the things that might not be ideal for a raffle could be wonderful contributions to our DDC costume wardrobe?'

'Leaping liquorice! Great idea!' said Hen trying on the purple ostrich hat.

'How do I look?' said Harry stumbling round in the pink stiletto heels. 'Super glam?'

Susie giggled and looked relieved. It was pretty difficult sometimes having a mother like Mrs Theodora Whistle-White.

'Time to get on with the rehearsal. Let's start with act two, scene one,' said Sophie. 'This is where Scrooge has just gone to bed and the Ghost of Christmas Past comes to visit him. We'll go on from there right through to the end if we have time. Everyone backstage.'

Backstage was behind some black material that Sophie's mum and dad had helped the girls hang up behind the stage. The stage was already in place and altogether it was beginning to look like a great little theatre. The only trouble was that it was pitch black backstage.

'I can't thee a thing,' cried Susie. 'It's tho thquary!'

John, who had been invited to join the club as lighting director volunteered to go and get a torch. As he ran across to the house he thought he caught sight of two shadowy figures behind the maple tree in the centre of the yard. 'Who's that?' he called out. But his words were swept away by a terrific wind that had blown up. He looked again but could see nobody. He shrugged it off, fetched the torch from his room and ran back to the barn.

'Just seen two ghosts outside,' he said cheerily.

'Don't John!' said Susie. 'I'm thcared of ghothts and that bit we've just done when the first ghotht appears is tho, tho thcweepy. I really don't like it - thpecially when Crethie ith being the Marley ghotht and keeps going on about howls and moans and cwanks and groans. It's tho, tho thquary!'

Susie started to cry.

'Susie,' said Beaky, 'you mustn't be frightened of the ghosts in the story. They're good ghosts coming to warn Scrooge and make him a better man.'

'Still pretty thquary all the same!' said Susie forcing a smile. But her smile turned to a look of fright.

'What's that creaking noise? Did you hear it?'

'Susie you're imagining things now.'

'Let's get on with the rehearsal.'

Hen was tip top as the Ghost of Christmas Past. She teased Scrooge by hiding and then popping out from nowhere!

```
Peep-po! Peep-po!
Look at me flitter and flow!
I sparkle and glitter
I revolve and dissolve
I come and I go!
Peep-po! Peep-po!
```

Scrooge became all confused ...

```
I see you! I see you!
No! Where did you go?
Disappeared! Abracadabra!
Puff! Like melted snow!
```

Susie, sitting out in the audience seats, laughed so hard till she cried. This wasn't a scary ghost at all. And Harry as the Ghost of Christmas Present was really jolly, leaping about the stage, waving the magic torch about and calling out:

```
Sprinkle it here, sprinkle it there
Spreading joy and merriment in the air!
```

Then came act four, scene one.

Only Sophie as Scrooge and Lou as the Ghost of Christmas Future were in the opening part of this scene so the others went to sit in the audience seats and watch.

John climbed up to the first floor to operate the lights.

'Everyone ready?' checked Cressie. 'Blackout John!'

John switched on his torch so he could see the dimmer pack. He then switched off the house lights. The children downstairs waited in the pitch-black. John shone his torch onto the dimmer switch and to his delight, crawling in and out of the controls, he spotted a large yellow insect that he had never seen before. What could it be? John completely forgot about the DDC waiting in the darkness down below as he peered closely at the little creature. It was some sort of beetle, pale primrose in colour with little red spots. It crawled slowly across the dimmer switch and down onto the table. Steadily but surely it moved on, unaware of the interest it was creating in the little boy whose nose was now a mere two inches from its back. Suddenly a cry from Sophie jolted John out of his magical insect world.

'John! What are you doing? We're all waiting!'

'Sorry. Technical hitch. Just checking on a bit of wildlife but ready now!' John called back.

The beetle scurried off.

Sighing John returned to his lighting duties, very slowly and carefully illuminating the stage with a green light. He turned the dimmer so gently that at first you could hardly see anything. Then slowly the dim outline of Scrooge lying in bed on stage emerged from the gloom. To Susie's horror a black figure appeared at the back of the stage.

She screamed!

'Ssshh Susie!' said Cressida. 'It's only Lou dressed up as the Ghost of Christmas Future.'

'Thorry! Thorry!' whispered Susie.

John turned up the green light a little more leaving the stage dimly lit.

Are you the Ghost of Christmas Yet to Come?
asked Scrooge in a terrified voice.

The ghost only lifted its arm and beckoned.

Ghost of the Future!
cried Scrooge.

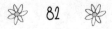

```
I fear you more than any spectre
    I have seen.
But as I know your purpose is to do me good
And as I hope to live to be another man
    from what I was
I am prepared to bear you company
And do it with a thankful heart.
Will you not speak to me?
```

The ghost kept its eerie silence and kept beckoning.
Scrooge rose from his bed to follow when he froze.

From the gloom behind the Ghost of Future had
appeared two *more* ghostly figures.

Scrooge knew that the Ghost of Future was Lou
dressed up. But who were the other two who had
appeared from nowhere... ?

It could only be one thing ...

... *real ghosts!*

The children in the audience sat frozen with fear,
unable to move. The Ghost of Christmas Future
turned to lead Scrooge off stage and was confronted
by the sight of two terrifying figures, white floaty
beings, beckoning just as he had done. The silence
was shattered as Lou let out the most piercing scream.

'Ghosts!' she screamed and rushed off stage.

'Turn the lights on John!' yelled Sophie.

Above all the commotion was the sound of Susie crying, 'Help! Help! Real ghothts! Help! Help!'

John, all alone up in the lighting gallery, had felt a shiver run down the back of his spine when he had seen the real ghosts appear on stage. He had watched, mesmerised in horror. Only Sophie's shouting to turn on the lights had brought him back to his senses. Trembling he reached for the house light switch and suddenly the whole of The Barn Theatre was bathed in glorious, bright white light.

'Into the house!' cried Beaky.

The children raced out of The Barn Theatre back to Sophie's house, barged through the door, and into the kitchen where they stood puffing and panting and trying to catch their breath.

Susie was sobbing uncontrollably.

'Those were real ghothts. I know they were! *The barn is haunted*!'

Sophie had been shocked by the sight of the apparitions but now back in her cosy kitchen it seemed impossible that real ghosts could have appeared - especially when her mum came in to see why everyone had charged into the kitchen in such chaos.

'We saw two howwible ghothth!' wailed Susie, still trembling.

'Two ghosts?' said Sophie's mum. 'I thought there were at least four in *A Christmas Carol*.'

'No. These ones were real,' said Cressida seriously.

'If there are some real ghosts out there I want to see them,' said Sophie's mum smiling. 'Anyone brave enough to come with me?'

Sophie's mum led the way across to The Barn Theatre with Sophie, Cressida, John, Harry and Beaky following cautiously. Hen and Abby stayed in the house to look after Lou and Susie who were still terrified.

'Right-ho. Where were these ghosts?' asked mum.

'They came from backstage,' said Beaky, hardly daring to look.

Mum went backstage. She looked behind all the curtains, under the stage and inside the props cupboard.

'There's nothing or nobody here,' she called.

'But ghosts wouldn't leave anything anyway would they. They just sort of disappear into thin air ... just like ... ghosts.'

'Hmm,' said mum. 'I think you must have been imagining things. Why don't you go and get the others and finish the rehearsal. You don't want them to go home frightened or thinking The Barn Theatre *is* haunted. I'll stay and watch. That should scare off any ghosts that might want to come back!'

'Thanks mum!' said Sophie relieved.

John went to fetch the others. Just as he went across the yard he remembered how he had seen those two shadowy figures lurking in the dark earlier on. This time he spent no time looking but ran into the house as fast as he could, thinking that he would tell Sophie about it later. Right now he had to encourage Lou and Susie to come back into The Barn Theatre to finish the rehearsal.

Mum switched all the lights on in The Barn Theatre and everyone began to feel more confident. She took Lou and Susie on a tour backstage, checking under the stage again and in the prop cupboard so that they could see they were empty.

Sophie decided that they would just rehearse the final act with Scrooge waking up, a changed man, and shouting out,

```
What? Awake! Christmas Day!
Merry Christmas! Merry Christmas!
I am as light as a feather!
I am as happy as an angel!
I am as giddy as a drunken man!
A Merry Christmas to everybody!
```

and being so jolly that everyone felt happy by the end and had almost forgotten about ghosts.

After the final scene everyone bowed and mum clapped. She found she was not the only one clapping. A few of the other parents had crept in including

Abby's father, Farmer Bagwash and Cressida's father, Tim Stack.

'Wonderful,' cried Sophie's mum. 'Quite magical! Isn't it marvellous how Scrooge changes from being such a mean spirited, bullying miser to a wonderful, warm-hearted fellow! It just goes to show that there's more to life than money.'

Farmer Bagwash and Tim Stack exchanged looks.

'Sometimes though,' said Tim, almost to himself, 'it does help to have an extra bob or two.'

The Ghost Hunt

School the next morning was agog with talk of
The Barn Theatre ghosts.

'Ooooooh!' said Elsa and Rosalie racing around
the playground. 'Nobody will want to come to your
play now that we know your barn is haunted!'

'It's not haunted,' retorted Sophie angrily. 'How do
you know about the ghosts anyway?'

'I know all about it because my baby sister, Lou
was up all night bawling her eyes out saying she was
frightened of the ghosts she had seen at The Barn
Theatre!' said Elsa, triumphantly.

'Is that true, Lou?' asked Sophie crossly.

'I'm sorry Sophie. I know I shouldn't have said but
I woke in the middle of the night and I kept
imagining those two horrible ghosts we saw. I was
so scared mum had to come and sleep in my room
with me.'

'See!' said Elsa to the gathering crowd of
schoolchildren. 'Lou did see some ghosts at The Barn
Theatre. It *is* haunted. None of us want to come and
see your play now Sophie and Cressida!'

Elsa and Rosalie ran off ran round the playground
making ghostly sounds and chasing and frightening
the little ones.

'Horrible girls!' said Sophie furious.

'Don't worry Lou,' said Cressida. 'To be honest I was a bit frightened, but I'm sure we must have imagined it. Let's have another practice tonight and I bet no ghosts will turn up.'

Sophie and Cressida wrote a note to all the members of the DDC.

URGENT and TOP SECRET
Come to a DDC meeting
TONIGHT 6.00

By six o'clock they had all gathered in The Barn Theatre. The house lights were on and Sophie had asked mum if they could have a plate of biscuits and some hot chocolate to make everyone feel happier.

Cressida started the meeting.

'Last night we all got a bit of a fright and now Elsa and Rosalie are trying to scare people and stop them coming to our play by saying The Barn Theatre is haunted. We've got to sort this out. Is anyone frightened now?'

The children looked around the barn. They had already started decorating it for the Christmas performance. Bright tinsel and jolly paper chains hung from the beams. Forty seats were laid out in rows with decorated numbers ready for the audience. There were the props bursting out of the props cupboard. There was a lucky dip barrel in one corner filled with lucky dip prizes. There was the raffle table with a sign saying 'Raffle Prizes'. There was the refreshments table and a beautifully decorated poster created by Lou.

There was their royal patron King Arthur smiling at them looking brave and happy with a festive bunch of holly dangling from his crown.

'It's more fun than frightening,' said Susie bravely.

'Yes,' nodded Beaky, tapping her nose. 'There is nothing to be frightened of now.'

'I think we must have imagined those ghosts last night,' added Lou, trying to convince herself.

'Now we're drinking hot chocolate I think it's the best place in the world!' said John.

The children sat around laughing and joking until they were all in very good spirits.

Suddenly Lou screeched ...

... *'Look!'*

There above, in the lighting gallery, were the two shadowy ghosts they had seen the night before!

Susie started screaming and wouldn't stop.

'Who are you?' shouted Sophie.

There was no answer.

The ghosts stood still, beckoning.

To the other children's amazement Sophie leapt to her feet and dashed over to the rickety staircase and started to climb up towards the ghosts! The ghosts, seeing her approach, turned as if to fly away. Sophie, trembling and dreading what she might see, peeped up through the hole in the first floor.

She saw ... nothing! The ghosts had vanished.

All was silent save a creaking sound coming from the far end of the barn.

The Forbidden Door, which she had never seen open before, was now unlatched and swinging on its rusty hinges, blowing back and forth in the wind!

Despite her fear and hammering heart Sophie crept forwards towards the door ...

She remembered her promise to her father *never, never* to open The Forbidden Door. She remembered the treacherous drop to the ground below. But why was the door open now? She crept closer and closer and very, very cautiously peered out ...

... and she saw ...

... NOTHING!

Only an empty blackness. No ghosts at all. They had disappeared. Could they really be spirits or spectres? She *had* to find out.

'Quick!' shouted Sophie, running back across to the staircase and clambering down to the others. 'They've disappeared out of The Forbidden Door.'

'But The Forbidden Door only leads to fresh air!' gasped John. 'They can't have got out of there unless...'

He left his sentence half finished. Only real ghosts could vanish into fresh air!

'Go and get your torch John and meet us outside at the back of the barn. We've got to investigate.'

Sophie had been so surprised by the sight of the two ghosts that she had forgotten to be frightened and led the way, ignoring Susie's protests of being scared, round to the back of the barn.

'Aaah!' screamed Susie. 'A ghost!'

'It's only me silly,' said John emerging from the dark and shining his torch.

'Right,' said Sophie. 'Shine it up at The Forbidden Door first.'

John shone the torch up and all the children looked at the creaky old door moving backwards and forwards in the wind.

'Now shine it straight down on the ground.'

Sophie crouched down on the ground to where the torch was shining and started to look carefully amongst the long grass.

'What are you looking for?' asked Susie in a frightened whisper.

'Clues!' said Sophie.

'But ghosts don't leave clues. They just disappear.'

'These ones leave clues,' said Sophie, triumphantly. 'Look!'

She pointed to two small muddy holes in the ground. The others stared.

'What's so interesting about them?' asked Abby

'They're little holes made by a ladder!'

'You mean somebody put a ladder here and climbed up through the door above,' said Hen getting the picture.

'And then tried to spook us by pretending to be ghosts!' added Harry.

'They could be ghoth prints,' said Susie who was still feeling very nervous.

'They could,' said Sophie. 'But I think they're more likely to have come from a ladder. I know its dark but let's all have a hunt around. See if our visitors hid the ladder somewhere before making their escape.'

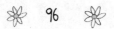

The children looked everywhere but there was no sign of a ladder.

'I think we should go back into the barn and finish our rehearsal,' said Cressida. 'We were getting on so well and we can't let two silly ghosts ruin it for us.'

'Do you think they were ghothts?' asked Susie, frightened again.

'No, definitely not!' said Cressida, sounding more confident than she felt.

But if they weren't ghosts *who were they*?

And why would they have been trying to frighten the Daisy Drama Club?

Pink Lollipop

Farmer Bagwash was going berserk. His little ladder that he used for all sorts of odd jobs had gone missing. He knew he had had it the day before because he used it to climb up the wall of the milking parlour to fix a bloomin' broken window. Now the bloomin' guttering was in danger of falling off the bloomin' cowshed and he couldn't fix it because he couldn't find the bloomin' ladder. And if he didn't fix the bloomin' gutterin' the bloomin' cowshed might come

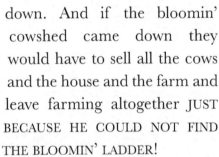

down. And if the bloomin' cowshed came down they would have to sell all the cows and the house and the farm and leave farming altogether JUST BECAUSE HE COULD NOT FIND THE BLOOMIN' LADDER!

'Dear, dear!' said Mrs Bagwash trying to console him. She was used to her husband's flustered outbursts. 'Why don't you go for a walk with Lollipop? It might calm you down.'

'Berwooomph!' exploded Farmer Bagwash.

This strange whistling sound used to shock Mrs Bagwash when they were first married but now she found it a useful sign that her husband was reaching bursting point!

'Berwooomph!' he repeated careering round the kitchen like a bull in a china shop. 'A walk! Do you know how much work I've got to do this afternoon?'

'You've been working since six o'clock this morning without a break. It's a lovely day and I think it would do you good,' persisted Mrs Bagwash gently.

'Do me good! Do me good! I know what does me good. Berwooomph I do! Having my tools at the ready! Come on Lollipop. Let's go on a walk to find the bloomin' ladder.'

'A walk? What a good idea!' said Mrs Bagwash smiling.

Farmer Bagwash set off with Lollipop, his sheep dog, scampering at his side. He turned into Goose Lane. He spotted Tim Stack, Cressida's father, perched up a ladder, painting the window frames of Mrs Whistle-White's house a violent pink.

'Jolly colour, what!' called out Farmer Bagwash, thinking how ghastly it looked.

'I'm glad you approve. Pink has always been my favourite. I chose this particular shade myself. It's called Puff Puff Pink if you're interested,' interjected Mrs Theodora Whistle-White grandly, as she popped up from behind a rose bed in her garden, where she had been deadheading. 'I say Farmer Bagwash! What *are* you doing?'

It appeared Farmer Bagwash had suddenly gone completely mad. With Lollipop at his heels, he leapt over Mrs Whistle-White's pride and joy of a privet hedge, which had been carefully clipped into shapes of peacocks, ran up to Tim Stack and almost exploding, shouted, 'Berwooomph! My bloomin' ladder! You're up my bloomin' ladder!'

As he spoke Farmer Bagwash shook the ladder vigorously.

The ladder wobbled so violently that Tim dropped his bucket of Puff Puff Pink paint over the barking Lollipop. Lollipop found herself covered from head to tail in the horrible, sticky pink stuff! In fright she tore around at top speed leaving bright pink paw marks all over Mrs Whistle-White's stone patio.

'Lollipop!' shouted Farmer Bagwash, forgetting the ladder. But Lollipop was very upset by the goo all over her fur and continued to bark and race around in circles in panic.

'My patio!' screeched Mrs Whistle-White. 'It's ruined! Ruined! Ruined!'

In the crisis only Tim kept his head. Tim loved animals and was horrified to see poor Lollipop so distressed. He jumped to the ground and crouched down. 'Come here Lollipop. Here Lolly,' he called gently and whistled.

Lollipop, sensing help was at hand, went directly to Tim. Tim stroked and patted her, not minding the paint going all over himself. Lollipop soon calmed down.

'Farmer Bagwash, would you like me to carry her back to Hawthorne Cottage and get her cleaned up?' asked Tim kindly. 'I'll drop her back at your farm later on.'

'Thank you, Tim, I would be most grateful.' Farmer Bagwash watched Tim walk off with Lollipop in his arms. 'Good with animals, that man,' he thought, as he calmed down.

'But what about my patio?' wailed Mrs Whistle-White. 'Look at it! Just look! It's gone pink! This is all *your* fault Farmer Bagwash for leaping over my fence like a wild horse, then shouting at poor Tim about the ladder.'

'Oh yes! The bloomin' ladder! Berwooomph! Of course the bloomin' ladder! I had completely forgotten. That man may be good with animals but I'm sorry to say Mrs Whistle-White he's also a... berwooomph... thief! That's *my* bloomin' ladder he's got there!'

'Thief, Farmer Bagwash? Thief! You really are the most ridiculous man. *I* found that ladder in my garden this morning. It had been thrown over my poor peacock hedge in the night by some wretched vandals. I merely suggested to Mr Stack that he may like to use it while he was painting my house. And when I find out who threw it over the hedge in the first place there will be big trouble!'

Farmer Bagwash picked up the ladder.

'Mrs Whistle-White. I'm sorry! I'm sorry! Berwooomph! This is my bloomin' ladder which someone stole from my farm yesterday. I'll take it home now if you don't mind and see if I can get to the bottom of the mystery!'

Sophie was round at Hawthorne Cottage helping Cressida pack all her books into a large box.

'Only a week before we move,' sighed Cressie.

'It just won't be the same without you,' added Sophie, sighing even more loudly. 'But at least you're not moving until the day after we've done the play.'

'But that makes it even worse. I can't *wait* for the play to hurry up but I'm also *dreading* the next day and moving. I don't know whether I want the time to go quickly or slowly. Even worse, because we're moving just before Christmas we can't even decorate here. Usually by now we have the Christmas tree up with its pretty lights and tinsel everywhere. This year we've got nothing. It looks so bare and gloomy.'

The cottage did look forlorn.

'Cressie,' cried Sophie looking out of the window. 'Your dad's carrying a pink dog!'

'Ghosts - now pink dogs! I don't believe you!'

But Sophie was right. The girls rushed down to see what had happened to the poor sheepdog.

Tim was talking softly to Lollipop the whole time. It took a long time to wash the sticky paint off but at last Lollipop was back to her black and white fur.

'Poor Lolly,' said Tim 'She's had quite a shock but she looks happy enough now. And all because Farmer Bagwash thought I'd stolen his ladder!'

Sophie and Cressida gasped in amazement.

A stolen ladder!

Could that possibly be the ladder that the ghosts had used last night?

'Why did he think you had stolen the ladder, daddy?' asked Cressida shocked that anyone could think such a thing.

Tim explained how Mrs Whistle-White had found the ladder in her garden that morning and suggested he used it while he was painting her house.

'Mr Stack,' said Sophie. 'Would you like us to take Lollipop back to Farmer Bagwash for you?'

'That's very kind of you. Thank you. It'll let me get on with some packing. We'll be very sorry to leave this cottage and miss seeing you bounding about the fields Miss Lollipop,' he added patting Lollipop fondly.

The girls set off with Lollipop at their heels.

'Do you think it could be Farmer Bagwash's ladder that the ghosts used last night?' asked Cressida incredulously.

'It could be,' said Sophie. 'We need to investigate!'

The Disappearing Ladder

When the girls reached Rook Farm they had to squeeze themselves up against the yard fence as Abby came charging by on Pickle.

'Sorry!' yelled Abby as she tore past. 'Pickle and I are just practising posting a letter whilst riding a pony. It's one of my riding tests but I think he got a bit spooked by the letter! Pickle! Pickle! Slow down.'

Abby managed to calm Pickle down and was really pleased to see Sophie and Cressida and, of course, Lollipop, who was still looking a rather odd colour.

'Lollipop, you've got a pink glow!'

'We'll explain that later,' said Cressida. 'Right now we need your help. Have you got a tape measure?'

They followed Abby and Pickle over to Farmer Bagwash's workshop and after some rummaging around in various drawers, Abby found a well used tape measure.

'Now, where's the ladder that your father found today?'

'He's up a ladder right now mending the cowshed. Come with me.'

The girls found Farmer Bagwash up the ladder.

'Lollipop! You've bought Lollipop back,' cried Farmer Bagwash in delight when he saw his sheepdog. 'Who's a good girl then! Who's a good girl then!' he said patting the excited Lollipop. 'Your dad is bloomin' marvellous with animals, young Cressida. Should have seen the way he calmed poor Lollipop down when she got covered in that ghastly pink paint. Bloomin' marvellous it was. You don't often find chaps with those sort of skills around these days.'

'And he won't be around for much longer, Farmer Bagwash,' added Sophie.

'And why's that?' asked Farmer Bagwash, still making a fuss of Lollipop and only half listening.

'Because he's got to move out of Hawthorne Cottage on Saturday. And all his family. They're going to Ditch. But you know all about that, Farmer Bagwash, it being your cottage.'

Cressida looked horrified at Sophie's frank talking. Abby, who had known nothing about it until that moment was shocked.

'But why have they got to move? Cressie is one of my best friends and we need her to run the DDC!'

Farmer Bagwash was flustered.

'I... I.... Berwooomph! Now look here! Children shouldn't interfere with adult business. And business is business. I have an agreement with the Stacks and they know that and I know that and we all know that and that's that. And that's all there is to say about that! Berwooomph!'

Farmer Bagwash climbed down the ladder and stormed inside.

'I'm really sorry ...' began Abby.

'Ssssh!' interrupted Cressida. 'I know what you're going to say and it's not your fault. It's not your dad's fault either. We just haven't got enough money. So we're going. It's as simple as that.'

Cressida could be quite philosophical at times.

'Now to more practical things. Abby, have you got the tape measure?'

Abby produced the tape measure and Cressida measured the width of the bottom of the ladder. Eleven and a half inches.

'Thanks Abby. See you at the dress rehearsal on Thursday. Our last practice before the real thing so don't be late!'

'Did you hear that Pickle? Best behaviour on Thursday. I don't want any pony pranks making me late for the dress rehearsal.'

Pickle looked at Abby.

Pony pranks?

What a good idea!

Back at The Old Farmhouse Cressida measured the gap between the two muddy holes which were in the ground directly below The Forbidden Door.

'Eleven and a half inches!' said Cressida triumphantly. 'That means it's pretty likely that whoever was trying to scare us the other night had stolen Farmer Bagwash's ladder and used it to climb up onto the first floor of The Barn Theatre!'

'Super sleuth detective work Cress. Now we've got to catch them!' said Sophie. 'Whoever it is is playing a pretty mean trick and really frightening some of us. I mean those of us who think the ghosts are real.'

'Do you think it could be real ghosts?' asked Cressida cautiously.

'No I don't. Not really. And anyway real ghosts wouldn't bother to steal a ladder. They would just sort of float up if they wanted to get anywhere.'

'And if they aren't ghosts they won't be coming back through The Forbidden Door because they haven't got the ladder anymore,' added Cressie logically.

'You're right,' said Sophie. 'Still, we'd better keep a sharp look out!'

Dress Rehearsal Drama!

The dress rehearsal was a disaster. It started off well enough. Lou had been sewing like mad and collecting items and hanging them up from the costume beam in the barn. Everyone was thrilled with her work.

'Only three more items needed,' she said efficiently checking everything off her list. 'Abby, have you got that holly to make the Ghost of Christmas Present's headdress?'

'Yes, only Pickle trod on it so some leaves got a bit squashed but I think it just about survived.'

'Harry and Hen, did you bring the black material for the Ghost of Christmas Future's outfit?'

'Ooooh!' said Susie squealing in fright as she saw a monstrous shape swaying on the stage.

'Only us!' said Harry and Hen, throwing off the big black sheet of cotton they had been hiding under.

'You thcared me!' said Susie, nervous. 'I hope thoth ghothth aren't going to come back.'

Ghosts! Everyone felt a bit jittery so Lou went swiftly on. 'Beaky, did you remember to bring your grandpa's old waistcoat?'

Beaky tapped her nose. 'Of course!'

Grandpa Albert had been very generous in lending the cast all sorts of items: three jackets, a cravat, a

walking stick and even the splendid top hat he had worn on the day he had married his beloved Ethel.

'Happy days! Happy days!' he said as he handed it over to Beaky.

'Are you *sure* grandpa?' Beaky had thought the tall, silky hat rather too precious to use in the play.

'Sure? Of course I'm sure! It will be a thrill to see it in action instead of sitting on a high shelf doing nothing at all!'

Under Lou's guidance everyone tried on their costumes. She measured and pinned and tacked material until all the costumes were to her satisfaction.

'A few more stitches here and there and we should be finished,' she mumbled, her mouth full of pins.

Finally Lou stood back to have a look at the cast.

'Fabulous!' she said in her best wardrobe mistress voice. 'You all look fabulous!'

'Fabulouth!' echoed Susie, trying to feel brave.

It was time for the dress rehearsal to begin.

In costume everyone felt so much more part of their part that to begin with Beaky hardly had to prompt anyone. Everyone had learnt their lines well. But when it got to the scene with the Ghost of Christmas Future, Susie started getting scared again. She could not stop looking over her shoulders, under her chair, behind the staircase and begging Sophie to check that there was nothing lurking backstage.

'I'm just tho, tho thcared thoth ghoth are going to come back,' she cried.

'So am I,' admitted Lou.

After that everyone was jittery and Beaky was kept busy prompting nearly every line. Nobody could remember anything!

'These ghosts are causing trouble even though they are only here in spirit!' said Sophie, which made everyone laugh, if a little nervously.

At last they got to the final scene. It had been a messy, chaotic performance.

'They do say,' said Cressida as they practised the bow for a second time, 'that a bad dress rehearsal means a good performance!'

'In that case,' said Beaky cheering up and tapping her nose, 'it should be a *wonderful* performance!'

The next day in the playground Abby Bagwash, her hair wild and Bertie sticking out of her shirt pocket, rushed up to Sophie and Cressida.

'You'll never guess what,' she said breathlessly, 'it's daddy's ladder. It's gone missing again!'

Sophie and Cressida looked at Abby in amazement.

Abby, who seemed very anxious, went on. 'And that's not all, is it Bertie! My dad's really mad. He's 'berwooomphing' about all over the place! I haven't told him about the ghosts. He thinks your dad, Cressida, has taken his silly ladder! I know he hasn't, of course, but you know what my dad is like. Yesterday he was going on about how wonderful your dad was with animals. Today he thinks your dad's a rotten thief! What shall I do? I don't think he'd believe my story if I said it was ghosts!'

Cressie was shocked that anyone could accuse her dad of stealing and she could also see how upset Abby was. 'Don't worry Abby - or you Bertie. Of course my dad would never steal anything.'

'It must be the so called ghosts who are trying to frighten us,' said Sophie angrily.

'But why would they steal the ladder again?'

'Because,' said Sophie thinking aloud, 'they must be coming back up through The Forbidden Door.'

'But when?' said Abby. 'Our performance is *tomorrow* night!'

'Exactly!' said Sophie.

'You don't think,' said Cressida tentatively, 'that they might want to ruin our play by scaring off the audience?'

'That's *exactly* what I think,' said Sophie. 'Our only solution is to lay a trap!'

Sophie's Great Idea

That night was stormy. Above the howling wind there was the sound of a loud, urgent knocking on the door of The Old Farmhouse. It was Cressida. She was completely drenched, her hair plastered to her face and she was shivering and shaking but as soon as she saw Sophie she started blurting out her story, still standing on the doorstep in the pouring rain.

'Come in,' urged Sophie and pulled her friend into the house.

Minutes later Cressida was sitting on Sophie's bed, wrapped in a great, big fluffy towel while her soggy clothes dried on the aga downstairs. Her teeth were still chattering from the cold but she managed to tell Sophie about all the dramas going on at Hawthorne Cottage. Farmer Bagwash, bright red in the face and with Lollipop at his heels, had been round berwooomphing and shouting, demanding that Cressie's dad must give him back his ladder or he would call the police.

'Of course dad doesn't know anything about the silly ladder!' said Cressida crossly, her teeth still chattering. 'So he just told Farmer Bagwash to have a look around if he liked and take the ladder if he could find it. Most of our stuff is packed up so it was easy to see that dad wasn't hiding it anywhere. Mum told Farmer Bagwash to come back when he'd calmed down but he just left muttering how you couldn't trust anyone these days. It was quite funny though because just as Farmer Bagwash was leaving Lollipop bounded up to dad and gave him a big lick as if she was saying 'don't worry'!'

'We've got to get to the bottom of the mystery though Cress. We'll think of something.'

'Funny that our big night is tomorrow night with THE ACTUAL PERFORMANCE and here we are talking about ladders and ghosts! I didn't imagine it to be like this!'

'No you're right Cress. Come on let's do something positive about the performance and we might get some ideas on how to solve our problems. Cressie, you're still shivering! Let's go and sit in the kitchen. It's really cosy in there.'

The girls went downstairs and sat round the kitchen table drinking steaming mugs of hot chocolate.

'How about tickets? How many have we sold?'

'Here's the list of people who have bought tickets. It's a bit messy because everyone in the DDC kept writing names then crossing them out and writing other names. How many actual tickets sold do you think there are?'

Cressida counted.

'Twelve.'

'Only *twelve*! Are you sure? That's a disaster and super disappointing when we've got room for at least forty!' said Sophie shocked. 'I bet that horrible Elsa and her creepy friend Rosalie have been going round telling everyone that The Barn Theatre is haunted to frighten them off!'

'Perhaps people just don't know it's on,' suggested Cressida warming up.

'They must be blind as bats then. We've put up millions of posters all over the village!'

Sophie's mum came into the kitchen.

'Perhaps you should do a leaflet and drop it into all the nearby houses. You might get one or two more people to come along.'

'Great idea mum!'

'Let's do it now,' said Cress.

'You can't go out again! You're only just dry.'

'I want to do something otherwise I'll start thinking about that bloomin' ladder again!' said Cress imitating Farmer Bagwash. 'Berwooomph!' she added for effect!

So the girls wrote a leaflet out ten times each and then set off in wellies and waterproofs and huddling under a giant black umbrella which caught all the gusts of wind and got stuck in bushes and trapped by overhead branches. Despite the wind, rain and troublesome umbrella they posted their leaflets through letterboxes up and down the village.

When the girls got back to The Old Farmhouse Sophie beckoned mysteriously to Cressida. 'I've had an idea for a ghost trap! Come on. We're going to need King Arthur's help!'

The girls dashed across to The Barn Theatre and switched on the house lights. There was King Arthur sitting patiently on the back row.

'If those so called ghosts come tomorrow night and try and ruin our play we'll be ready for them and give them a nasty fright!' said Sophie. 'Help me get Arthur upstairs onto the lighting floor.'

With great difficulty the girls carried King Arthur up the rickety staircase and set him down on a chair.

'Now let's tie this rope around his waist and then throw the other end over that wooden beam up there. Can you catch the other end, Cress?'

'Got it!'

'Great! I'm just going to get something from the kitchen.'

In a few seconds Sophie was back with a bag of flour and an old white sheet.

'Could you go over to The Forbidden Door Cress and shut your eyes. Don't open them until I say so.'

Cressida did as her friend asked. After a few minutes Sophie switched off the house lights.

'Open your eyes now Cress!'

Cressie opened her eyes. To begin with she saw nothing. It was completely dark and silent save the howling of the wind outside and the relentless drumming of the rain on the barn roof. Eventually she became aware of a faint green light growing stronger and out of the gloom she could see a mysterious, ghostly figure. With a terrifying howl the

figure flew into the air, shooting up to the eaves as if flying! There was a bang and the air was suddenly filled with a spooky white dust. There was another bang as the ghost flew dramatically back to the ground landing at Cressida's feet. Cressie was really scared!

'Sophie!' she yelled, 'What's happening?'

Sophie turned on the house lights.

'Yes! Brilliant! Bullseye!'

Sophie was leaping around in delight - until she saw how much she had scared Cressida. 'Sorry Cress! I didn't mean to scare you, but I just wanted to test my anti-ghost plan out on someone and you were the tip top best person!'

'Thanks a lot Sophie!' said Cressida. Looking at the figure on the floor she realised it was only King Arthur with a white sheet tied around him like a cloak. 'But where did the dust come from?'

'I put a small bag of flour on the beam up there,' said Sophie pointing upwards, 'and when I pulled the rope to make King Arthur fly into the air he went right up to the beam, knocked the bag over and sent flour everywhere. Hopefully it'll go all over whoever is trying to frighten us. I'll put much more flour up there when it's the real thing!'

Cressida was smiling now.

'Well even though I really knew it was only you and King Arthur it was still pretty scary. Hopefully it's just what we need to catch our ghosts!'

Trapped!

The day of THE ACTUAL PERFORMANCE dawned bright and blustery. After school all the members of the DDC raced back to Sophie's house for a cast tea but everyone was much too excited to eat very much.

'Let's practise the spirit song,' said Hen.

'Good idea,' agreed Harry. 'Ready everyone?'

```
Humbug! Humbug! Humbug! Hummmmmmmm!
Spirits of the darkness!
Ghosts of the night! Oooooooooh!
Ghouls of the shadows!
Sprites in flight! Oooooooooh!
With howls and moans! Ooooooh!
With clanks and groans! Oooooooh!
Turn that grasping, clutching,
    covetous old sinner
From grimness, grief and folly.
Spirits! Make him JOLLY!
Scrooooooooge!
```

'It's thcwary,' said Susie shyly when they'd finished. 'You don't think those real ghosts will come back tonight do you?'

'Don't worry,' said Sophie winking at Cressie. 'We've got a surprise for them if they do!'

'It's five o'clock,' said Cressida. 'We ought to be ready by six o'clock when the audience will start turning up. Time to put on our costumes!'

Lou, Harry and Hen had brought all the costumes across from the barn and Lou supervised the dressing. They were just about to start adding face paint when there was a knock on the door. It was Uncle Max.

'Hello chaps! Thought you might like to use this. A gift from me. Well the truth is the charming make up artist at Stibblewick Theatre was having a clear out and I exchanged this lot for ten jars of my homemade jam, five pots of chutney and a barrel load of apples. Cheerio chaps!'

Uncle Max disappeared as quickly as he had appeared, leaving a large box on the doormat. The girls carried it in and put it down on the kitchen table.

'Open it! Open it!' cried Abby excited.

Beaky lifted the lid. The box was jammed packed with all sorts of bottles and brushes, lotions and potions, pencils and powder puffs.

'What is all this stuff?' asked Abby perplexed.

'It'th make up,' said Susie. 'I know all about thith. My mum hath tonth and tonth of make up.'

Lou was so excited she thought she might faint!

'It's not *just* make up Susie. It's stage make up!'

Lou dived into the box and started pulling out all sorts of weird and wonderful things.

'Look at this! Cake eye liner, aluminium glitter, anti shine powder, a pack of cold foam noses, Buster's blood capsules, phosphorescent cream foundation, long lash mascara.'

'Mum's got thome of that,' interrupted Susie.

'Oooh, showgirl eyelashes too - and look at this a packet with two fresh scratches. Oh please, please could I do the make up?'

'Can I be your athithtant?' asked Susie.

Soon Lou and Susie had set up a make up table and set to work.

Cressida and Sophie asked if they could be made up first as they had a special mission to undertake before the show started.

'Right Susie,' said Lou. 'Start by giving Cressie a green face for Jacob Marley. I'll give Sophie wrinkles.'

Susie did as she was told. When she had finished she looked critically at the green faced Cressida.

'I think she just looks thick,' said Susie doubtfully. 'I'm going to give her some more details.'

Cressida was worried about the details but Susie, who had watched her mother putting on make up on more occasions than she would wish to remember, proved to be very skillful. Meanwhile Lou was in her element and transformed Sophie into a very convincing Scrooge. As soon as they were finished Lou called out, 'next please!' and set to work on Harry and Hen.

The moment had come. Sophie and Cressida sneaked out of the house, over to the barn to put their ghost trap into action!

Sophie unlocked the barn door. She used her torch instead of the switching on the house lights.

'If those ghosts are going to turn up it'll be any minute now. There's no way they could have opened the main door because it's been locked since our last rehearsal. I'll lock it again now. The only way in is through The Forbidden Door. Let's go up and hide.'

With thumping hearts the girls went up to the lighting floor. Sophie shone her torch at King Arthur who was sitting happily with his white sheet tucked around him and then up to the beam where there was a large bag of flour perched precariously.

'All ready for action?' she whispered to Cress. 'Let's crouch down here and see what happens.'

For five minutes they waited in silence in the pitch black. The sound of sharp tap of wood on wood made them jump. It came from the other side of The Forbidden Door! Then came the sound of footsteps climbing up a ladder. Seconds later and very, very slowly, with a soft, creaking noise The Forbidden Door swung open. A shadowy figure paused briefly, then entered and from its outline the girls could make out that it was beckoning to someone below. A second figure emerged and stepped in through The Forbidden Door.

'All clear,' whispered the first figure in a voice that seemed strangely familiar. 'There's no-one here yet.'

'Are you sure?' said the second figure.

'Sure as sure!' said the first. 'Now remember our plan. When the audience are sitting down and the play is about to begin we start howling. Loud as we can! The audience won't know whether it's part of the play or not but the DDC will think it's ghosts and run out crying. They'll make real fools of themselves and it'll ruin their show.'

'But it'll be worth it for the laugh!' added the second figure.

'Sssssh! What's that?'

'Someone's coming up the ladder!'

The two figures froze in horror. Sophie and Cressida could not believe their eyes when they saw *another* figure coming through The Forbidden Door.

Could *this* be a real ghost?

A huge, monstrous outline filled the whole opening. It was grunting like a wild beast! As it stepped through the door Sophie in her fright decided this was the moment for action.

'Now!' she hissed to Cressie.

Trembling Cressida turned on the dim green light. In the same instant Sophie pulled as hard as she could on the rope. The King Arthur 'ghost' leapt from his seat and flew dramatically across the room, and went sweeping up - 'BANG!', 'CRASH!' - hitting the beam.

A great cloud of white flour dust shot into the air as the white apparition completed it's flight by diving to the ground knocking over the two smaller figures,

flinging them to the ground as they let out almighty screams for help.

'Aaaaaah! Ghosts! The barn really *is* haunted! Let's get out of here! Help! Help!'

Somewhere amongst the high pitched screams Cressida heard a fearsome shout.

'What the blazes is going on?'

'Lights on! Lights on!' whispered Sophie urgently to Cressida.

'Right-ho! but don't let whoever it is know that we're here yet!' answered Cressida whose heart was beating nineteen to the dozen.

What was going on?

Who was the mysterious third figure?

Was it *really* a ghost?

Cressida turned on the house lights. Once the room was lit up it took all their efforts not to burst out laughing at the chaotic scene before them. Cressida pushed her knuckles into her mouth to stop herself and Sophie tried to muffle her giggles in her large Scrooge handkerchief!

There was the mean Elsa and nasty Rosalie covered in white flour, cowering in the corner staring in horror at King Arthur who was lying in an unkingly manner face down on the floor.

'Aaaaaah!' screamed Elsa terrified.

'Ghosts!' screeched Rosalie.

'Look!' yelled Elsa pointing at a giant covered in ghostly dust striding towards them, his black, foreboding eyes popping out of a deathly white skull-like face. His finger was pointing directly at the terrified Elsa and Rosalie.

'Berwooomph! YOU!' it bellowed in a deep and horrifying manner. 'It's YOU who've stolen the bloomin' ladder!'

From where they were hiding Cressida and Sophie could see that it was none other than Farmer Bagwash! But Elsa and Rosalie, crouched in the corner, were dazzled by the house lights, so they could only make out the outline of the figure.

'Berwooomph! You will pay for this,' went on Farmer Bagwash in fury, looking just like the terrifying Ghost of Christmas Future.

'Please forgive us!' cried out Elsa, trembling.

'Have mercy on us,' begged Rosalie, hardly able to speak for fear.

'It was only a joke!' added Elsa trying to save themselves.

'Joke! Berwooomph! Stealing is a serious offence that deserves dire and dastardly punishment!'

Elsa, now convinced that the figure really was a ghost fell sobbing and crying out that she was sorry and she knew she'd done wrong and that she'd never do anything wrong again and begged for forgiveness. Rosalie remained transfixed with horror.

Cressida whispered to Sophie, 'I think they've suffered enough.'

'A shame. I'm enjoying this but perhaps you're right,' said Sophie 'Come on. To the rescue!'

Sophie and Cressida stood up. But they had forgotten that they had stage make-up on; Cressida looked a ghostly green and Sophie was covered in wrinkles. Elsa let out a further ear-piercing scream,

'More ghosts! Aaaaaah!'

Rosalie sat stone still, too shocked to speak!

'Elsa! Rosalie! It's only us. Sophie and Cressida. And that isn't a ghost. It's Farmer Bagwash. And that's just our mascot, King Arthur!'

'Aaaaaah!' screamed Elsa inconsolable.

'Elsa! Please!'

At last Elsa calmed down.

'Sophie? Cressida? Farmer Bagwash?' she looked from one to another. 'No ghosts?'

'No ghosts,' repeated Cressida kindly.

'King Arthur?' said Elsa sounding alarmed again.

'He's just our royal patron, aren't you King Arthur,' said Sophie picking up King Arthur and putting him on a chair to give him some royal dignity.

'No ghosts!' said Farmer Bagwash. 'Worse! Berwooomph! Wicked thieves caught red handed!'

'Oh Farmer Bagwash! We're not thieves,' protested Rosalie sobbing. 'We were only borrowing your ladder. Please don't send us to prison.'

'What you've done is wrong. Very wrong! Very, very wrong! I'm afraid I'll have to inform the police and they can deal with you.'

'Oh please don't,' begged Elsa, horrified. 'We'll get

in the most terrible trouble.'

'A wrong's been done and in my book a wrong should be paid for!' said Farmer Bagwash stubbornly.

'What if they are innocent?' asked Cressida suddenly.

'Then I would have done a wrong by wrongly accusing them which I would admit would have been a wrong thing to do myself and I would have to pay for that wrong!' replied Farmer Bagwash.

'And do you think they should forgive you for wrongly accusing them?' continued Cressida. Sophie smiled. Cressida was up to something!

'Well, it depends how I paid them for my wrong. Accusing someone of stealing when they haven't is a very serious matter. It can blight someone's character so just saying sorry might not be enough. You've got to show you really mean it! Oh really! Berwooomph!' exploded Farmer Bagwash confused. 'Where is this getting us? I've caught these girls red handed so I know they're guilty. I'm accusing them right now of stealing my bloomin' ladder.'

'So if they stole it no one else did?'

'Of course not!'

'Not even my dad!'

'Of course not!'

'So do you think you were wrong to accuse him?'

'I … oh dear … perhaps I was a little hasty.'

'So now you are in the wrong with him?'

'I'll just have to say I'm sorry!'

'You just said that saying 'sorry' is not enough. You have to *show* that you mean it!'

'Berwooomph! For goodness sake young lady. You're tying me in knots! I'll say sorry and what's more I'll do something to show that I mean it! Heaven knows what! But I'll do it!'

'Thank you Farmer Bagwash,' said Cressida smiling at him. 'Don't forget that we're leaving the village tomorrow so you'll have to be quick.'

'Leaving the village? But why?'

'Don't you remember? Our lease on Hawthorne Cottage runs out tomorrow and we can't afford your rent. Still, I suppose daddy will be able to get some work painting and decorating when we get to Ditch.'

'Ditch! Is that where you're off to? But that's a dreadful place!'

'I know Farmer Bagwash. We're very sorry to be going and have been so happy in your lovely cottage. We're so grateful to you that we've been able to live there at all. But I do understand. Business is business and emotions can't get in the way!'

'Quite right! No, quite wrong! Your wrongly right, or is that rightly wrong? Oh berwooomph!'

Farmer Bagwash stormed off down the staircase.

'The play!' shrieked Sophie. 'We can't be late for curtain up! Rosalie, Elsa, you'd better come over to the house with us and get cleaned up.'

The two big girls, still sobbing, followed Sophie and Cressida out of the barn, across the yard and into The Old Farmhouse. Lou, who had just put on her spirit outfit, looked shocked when she saw her sister.

'Elsa! What are *you* doing here? And why are you covered in all that white stuff. You look as if you've seen a ghost! What's been going on?'

'It's a long story, Lou,' replied Sophie before Elsa could say anything. 'Put it this way – we will not be having any more visits from real ghosts!'

Sophie showed Elsa and Rosalie the bathroom where they did their best to get rid of the flour.

'I'm really sorry,' said Elsa in a quiet voice.

'So am I,' added Rosalie.

'We didn't really mean to be so horrid,' went on Elsa. 'It's just that I thought the DDC was a brilliant idea and I wish I'd thought of it. I was just jealous. I realise how horrid I've been now. I'm sorry. Anyway I'll never be able to do anything fun like set up a DDC because I'll be in prison instead!'

And with that Elsa burst out crying.

Sophie felt very sorry for her.

❀ 135 ❀

'Tell you what,' said Sophie kindly, 'why don't you help us tonight. You and Rosalie could sell the tickets and show people to their seats. And at the interval you could do the lucky dip and raffle and help mum on the refreshments table. How about that?'

Through her tears Elsa smiled. She had had a nasty shock.

'We'd like to do that. That's if you can trust two burglars with the ticket money!'

'You bet!' said Sophie and the three girls went downstairs ready for the show to begin!

Chaos and Calamity!

By six o'clock Elsa and Rosalie were sitting at the little table at the entrance to The Barn Theatre, under the sign 'Box Office' which Beaky had made, with Grandpa Albert's help and Lou had decorated most beautifully. Sophie and Cressida were still anxious about the number of people who would turn up but they shouldn't have worried. Elsa and Rosalie were kept very busy selling tickets and they were most particular about keeping track of all the money.

Soon the forty seats were full and still people were arriving! There was Grandpa Albert on the second row, Uncle Max at the back, and in the middle Tim and Polly Stack, Mr Gumtree, Farmer and Mrs Bagwash, Mr and Mrs Whistle-White and a long queue at the Box Office.

Sophie's mum and dad propped up some wooden planks on logs to make extra benches so there were enough seats for everyone to sit down.

Twenty-four adults and thirty-three children!

It was an incredible turnout.

Where had they all come from?

'It might be something to do with some phone calls Elsa made,' said Sophie's mum. 'She was ringing people and telling them that The Barn Theatre wasn't really haunted and that she was sorry for scaring them and that the play was going to be wonderful and that they'd got to come along or they would miss a real treat!'

'Good for Elsa,' said Cressida. 'She really is sorry. It must have been difficult for her to ring up all those people and tell them she'd been wrong.'

The audience were indeed in for a treat. The Barn Theatre looked magical! The DDC had decorated it with great swathes of holly and ivy hanging from the ancient beams. Sophie's dad had woven twinkling fairy lights amongst the festive greenery. Golden baubles turned gently, catching and dancing in the coloured lights, glistening tinsel sparkled and glinted. A wonderful, warm smell of cinnamon and nutmeg hung in the air from the mulled wine and above all the excited chatter came the sound of Christmas carols from the music system Sophie's dad had set up especially for the show.

By now all the members of the DDC were backstage.

'Three minutes to go,' whispered John. 'I'm going up to do the lights now.'

John crept out from backstage and made his way to the back of the ground floor theatre and up to the lighting gallery. He loved it up there. There were always plenty of insects and spiders. It was also a magnificent view. He could see the heads of the audience and the stage quite clearly. He glanced around at The Forbidden Door. No sign of any ghosts! He glanced at his watch. One minute to go. He looked down at the ticket office. Elsa was looking at her watch. She peeped outside to make sure that there were no latecomers, made sure everyone inside The Barn Theatre had a seat, then turned and gave John the thumbs up. John grinned and gave Elsa the thumbs up back.

Time to roll!

John switched off the fairy lights, which were acting as house lights, plunging The Barn Theatre into darkness. The audience went quiet, hushed in excited expectation.

Very, very slowly John turned up the first lamp to form a pool of green on the centre of the stage. There was a slight shaking of the black curtain at the back of the stage and then through the gap emerged the gloomy spectre of the ghost of Jacob Marley. As Cressida walked in deathly slow steps towards the middle of the stage, clanking the chains of sin that Jacob was forced to carry for all his sins made while alive on earth, she felt miles away from the sad, dismal character she was playing. Her character, Marley, was supposed to be miserable but Cressida felt like whooping with joy!

Here she was at last!

On stage in their own theatre playing to a packed audience.

WHAT A WONDERFUL FEELING!

In the deep, slow and mournful voice that she had practised a thousand times Cressie began.

I have a merry Christmas tale to tell.
So full of woe
A sad, sad jolly tale.
Dismal. Heart rendering.
But fear not... it does have a happy ending.
Though I speak, I am really dead.
As dead as bread gone stale.
As dead as a dead, dead door nail.
My name is Marley
      ... and I fear... I am a ghost!
But tonight,
      I am happily your miserable host.
The tale I have to tell is of a man
      generous in his meanness
Delighting in his own sadness.
A sack of sin upon his shoulders so huge ...
Our very own Ebenezer Scrooge!

Backstage the DDC booed loudly at the word 'Scrooge'. Now the play had began they were all enjoying themselves. By the time they reached the interval it was clear that the audience was enjoying themselves too.

As the applause died down and chatter took over, John turned on the fairy lights and went backstage to join the DDC.

'It's fantastic!' he enthused. 'Tiny Tim, you were brilliant. I heard some of the audience sniffling when you were so brave even though you were so ill.'

'Did you?' said Susie surprised. 'I have been thinking and thinking what it would be like to be Tiny Tim, with no money and cold at Chrithtmath and a bad leg too. Thometimeth it maketh *me* cry when I think about it too much tho I wathn't really acting. I was jutht *being* Tiny Tim.'

'That shows you are a naturally wonderful actress,' said Cressida.

Susie beamed.

'Anything else John?' asked Cressida.

'Yes! Beaky don't poke your nose round the curtain again. Everyone can see you.'

'I'm sorry,' said Beaky. 'I only did it once. Just to see who was here. It's *so* exciting I could burst!'

'Five minutes till we're off again,' said Sophie.

'Right-ho!' said John. 'I'd better get back to my lights. Break a leg!'

'Break a leg? What about *good luck*?'

'I don't think you are meant to wish an actor good luck,' said John. 'It brings bad luck so you say *break a leg* instead.'

'Break a leg!' whispered Harry to Hen.

'Break a leg!' whispered Hen to Harry.

It was dark backstage behind the black curtains. The DDC could hear the chatter of the audience then the clear voice of Elsa.

'Ladies and gentlemen. Please take your seats. The second half of *A Christmas Carol* will begin in one minute. That is one minute.'

The chattering died down. All was silent.

Suddenly there was a terrific scream from the audience. 'Waaaaaaaaaaah! There's a horrible, hairy beast under my chair. Waaaaaaaaaaah! '

Susie, backstage, recognised that voice. It was her mother, Mrs Theodora Whistle-White. No mistake. What was going on?

'Berwooomph!' came an explosion. Abby looked horrified. That was her father, Farmer Bagwash. No mistake. Had Bertie escaped? He was hardly a hairy beast! No Bertie was safely in her pocket. He was her lucky mascot! It couldn't possibly be Pickle could it? No. Pickle was safely in his stable. Unless her mischievous pony had escaped ... What could be the matter? Why was her father berwooomphing!

'Berwooomph! For heaven's sake calm down Mrs Whistle-White,' shouted Farmer Bagwash. 'It's no *beast*. Just Lollipop.'

'Lollipop!' squeaked Abby.

What could *Lollipop* be up to?

'Lollipop! Berwooomph! Down girl! Leave Mrs Whistle-White alone!'

But by now Mrs Whistle-White, who was wearing her big furry coat, was standing up on a chair. 'Waaaaaaaaaaah! Get the beastly beast away from me! Waaaaaaaaaaaah!'

Her screaming made Lollipop more and more excited. She tried to jump and grab what seemed to her to be a great, white furry bear! She ignored all cries from Farmer Bagwash to come away. Uttering an enormous 'berwooomph!' Farmer Bagwash made a dive for his dog, but Lollipop thinking it all a jolly game leapt out of the way just in time. Farmer Bagwash crashed to the ground, knocking Mrs Whistle-White's chair as he went, unbalancing her so that with a final, ear-piercing 'Waaaaaaaah!' she was tossed into the air and landed in a flurry of white fur, bang crash on top of the spread-eagled Farmer Bagwash!

Meanwhile Lollipop made her escape.

The audience tried to catch her but it was no good. She was thoroughly enjoying herself leaping over chairs, squeezing through legs and wriggling out of hands trying to grab her. Amidst all the hub bub she heard a low whistle.

'Here Lollipop. Come here Lolly.'

Backstage Cressida grinned. That was her dad, Tim Stack. No mistake. Lollipop, hearing Tim's quiet, calm voice forgot all about the big, furry Whistle-White monster and the game of chase, and bounded over to Tim. The dog gave Tim an affectionate lick then flopped herself at his feet, enjoying being patted and stroked.

The rest of the audience picked up fallen chairs, Mrs Theodora Whistle-White disentangled herself from Farmer Bagwash, everyone sat down and John, sensing the moment had come, turned off the fairy lights. It was quiet and dark.

The second half of *A Christmas Carol* began with a challenge for the jolly Ghost of Christmas Present - *to make Scrooge smile!* But as much as the ghost waved his magic torch about to spread Christmas merriment Scrooge refused to smile.

The ghost tried again.

Did you see that? A flicker of a smile?
the Ghost of Christmas Present asked the audience.

No you did not!

Sophie as the miserable Scrooge had to refuse to smile. Poor Sophie! Like Cressida playing Jacob Marley in the opening scene she was finding it jolly hard *not* to smile!

Oh yes we did!
cried the Ghost of Christmas Present

Oh no you did not
said Scrooge in bad temper.

Oh yes we did!
cried the Ghost of Christmas Present, this time with the audience yelling and joining in.

Oh no you did not!
replied Scrooge, furious.

Oh yes we did!

All right you rotten old eggs,
said Scrooge beaten,
You might have seen
    a tincy, wincy, incy smile
But remember my face is a No Smile Zone

It's grim and chiselled from No Smile Bone
A smile you may have seen but now it's gone!
... And it's not coming back!

Oh yes it is!
roared the Ghost of Christmas Present and the
audience.

Oh no it is not!
sulked Scrooge.

Oh yes it is!

Oh no it is not!

Oh yes it is!

Well if it does it'll be very quick
    and gone in a flash
snarled back Scrooge.

Now came the moment Harry had been dreading:
her LONG SPEECH.
    What if her mind went blank?
    What if she forgot all her words?
    The only think that stopped her running away and

never coming back was knowing Beaky was backstage sitting with the prompt's light and a script ready to prompt her if she did forget. Thank goodness for Beaky! She took a deep breath and in her Ghost of Christmas Present voice bellowed,

```
I see I have a challenge tonight!
So let's get going
    and spread the joyful light
And praise the Lord
    for his almighty generosity!
Look around!
```

Harry waved her torch pointing around the stage.

```
There's ... there's ...
```

Her voice faded. Her mouth felt dry and despite it opening and closing no words came out.

Her worst nightmare had come true!

Harry's mind had gone blank!

There's *what?*

What an earth came next?

'Come on Beaky, prompt me!' she prayed.

But poor Beaky, normally so organised and in control, was having a crisis. The prompt light had suddenly flashed on and off, then the bulb exploded and gone out!

'I can't see a thing!' whispered Beaky frantically.

Sophie, also on stage, stared at Harry willing her to remember. All Sophie could remember was her own next line which was 'Humbug!'

Harry kept on waving her magic torch thinking, thinking, thinking when she heard a hiss offstage.

```
Red - berries - in - rombosity,
```
It was Hen's voice.

The twins had practised and practised their lines together so Hen knew Harry's as well as Harry did herself. Harry nearly fainted in relief.

```
There's red berries in rombosity ...
```

```
Holly - and - ivy, - geese - and - game
```
whispered Hen.

  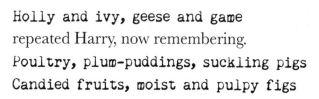

```
Holly and ivy, geese and game
```
repeated Harry, now remembering.
```
Poultry, plum-puddings, suckling pigs
Candied fruits, moist and pulpy figs
```

Barrels of oysters, luscious pears
Red-hot chestnuts,
    goosegogs covered in hairs.
Look at... look at...

 The words had gone again!

... folks - laughing - heartily ...
whispered Hen.

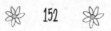

... folks laughing heartily,
    from er polished hearts
went on Harry
Choosing cinnamon and almond tarts.
Yo! Ho! Ho! What a laugh! What a hoot!
Come now!

Harry turned to face Scrooge. Her big speech was
over and she knew she knew the rest of her words.
Thank goodness for Hen!

Come now! I'm being rude.
Tell me Scrooge, your favourite food.

HUMBUG!
snapped Scrooge.

'Humbug' was a word Scrooge used to let off steam. He did NOT mean it was his favourite food!

Yo! Ho! 'Humbug'! What a joke ...
laughed the Ghost of Christmas Present, misunderstanding.

Humbug for you sir, it will be
And just for good measure give me a hand
Let's scatter some sweets all over the land!

Sweeeeeets!

The magic word!

Sophie and Harry started flinging out sweets to the audience. The younger children went crazy.
'Over here!'

'Over here!'

'Over here!'

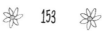

Grubby fingers stretched up to catch the flying chews, jellys, gums and fizzers. It was pandemonium. Children jumped up and down on their chairs, dived under chairs to find sweets on the floor and some started climbing up onto the stage.

Amongst the chaos Harry managed to send a fizzer flying over the black curtain to backstage.

'Leaping liquorice! Thanks Hen. You saved my life!' she yelled.

'That's what twins are for,' yelled back Hen.

The final sweet was thrown and the children scrambled back to their chairs, silenced by chewing, chomping jaws and excited to see what would happen next.

Backstage, where all was dark and quiet, Beaky, who had still not managed to get the prompt's light to work, was hopping around trying to change out of her spirit outfit into her Bob Cratchit jacket and trousers.

Poor Beaky!

She never liked to feel things were slipping out of her control. And worse was to come.

She tripped!

As she fell she reached out to grab something - *anything!* - to save herself. She snatched at the black backstage curtain which hid her from the stage and the audience. The curtain fell to the ground and Beaky, to her horror realised she was no longer backstage but *on* stage. Still hopping about, with trousers half on and half off, she was suddenly in the spotlight, the audience staring at her. She flushed bright red with embarrassment and hopped faster and faster trying to keep her balance and trying desperately to get the trousers on. But it was no good. In front of everyone she fell over. Everything was literally collapsing around her! Tears pricked her eyes.

But then a miraculous thing happened.

Grandpa Albert started to chuckle. The children on the front row started to giggle. Then the whole audience burst into laughter.

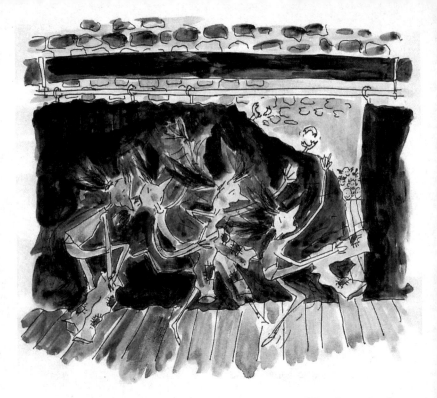

Grandpa Albert had saved the day! He thought it was funny and thinking about it, it was!

But what could Beaky do next?

Keep in character of course!

Scrooge was staring at her angrily so Beaky, tapped her nose, and said, 'I was wondering sir, if there would be a spare humbug going for your poor clerk?'

'Humbug? Certainly not!' said Scrooge. 'And put that curtain back this minute!'

With Hen's help Beaky hung up the curtain again. Beaky was back in control and *A Christmas Carol* continued!

Bagwash's Final 'Berwooomph!'

When the DDC made their final bow the audience clapped, cheered and the children at the front leapt up and down shouting for more so the DDC obliged and come back on stage three times for a another bow and another bow and another bow before disappearing finally backstage. Elsa and Rosalie rushed to congratulate them.

'Brilliant!' said Elsa.

'Fantastic!' said Rosalie.

'Here's all the money you've made and here's a list of what's what,' added Elsa handing Sophie the tin money box and a piece of paper with jottings and adding ups and a large total at the end.

'Leaping liquorice!' said Hen.

'Leaping liquorice times two!' said Harry.

'Tip top!' said Sophie. 'Now we can easily pay Uncle Max for the lights and dad for the stage and still have some left over towards our next production. That's if ...'

Sophie's voice faded away. In the excitement of the play she had forgotten that Cressida was leaving Wissop tomorrow! Sophie could never run the DDC on her own.

Just then Farmer Bagwash barged backstage.

'Berwooomph! I've got something to say to you girls!' he said.

'Oh no!' thought Elsa and Rosalie. 'I bet he's got the police outside and we are off to prison straight away!'

'Oh no!' thought Abby. 'I bet it's going to be something to do with naughty animals!'

'Oh no!' thought Cressida and Sophie. 'It bet it's something about having to leave Hawthorne Cottage tonight!'

Susie, who was feeling very confident after her fine performance as Tiny Tim, spoke up.

'Yeth, Farmer Bagwath, what ith it?'

'Firstly Elsa and Rosalie. I've been watching you this evening. I've seen how carefully you took the ticket money. I've observed how meticulous you were about checking the raffle money. I have decided that there is hope for you and that you could be honest and trustworthy girls. I've decided to give you one more chance. I will not say a word to anyone about the ladder incident. Shall we say it's a matter forgotten?'

'Oh, thank you Farmer Bagwash!' said the girls with great relief. Visions of days spent rotting in some dank, dark prison faded away. The future suddenly took on a rosy hue.

'As for you, young lady,' said Farmer Bagwash turning to face Cressida. 'You have made me think. Perhaps I have been a little hasty. I should never have accused your father of stealing. He's in fact, the most honest of men. I've just been having a chat with him and apologised. I have ... berwooomph!... been wrong!'

Abby's eyes nearly popped out of her head. She had never, ever heard her father admit to being wrong!

'Not only that but I could do with some help on the farm with the animals. I need a good chap. Someone that understands and cares for animals. Just like your father does, Cressida. So I've .... berwooomph! ... offered your father the job!'

'But Farmer Bagwash I know he'd love to work on a farm with animals but he couldn't possibly take the job. We're moving to Ditch tomorrow,' said Cressida.

'Hawthorne Cottage goes with the job!' replied Farmer Bagwash in a matter-of-fact voice.

'Hawthorne Cottage goes with the job!' Cressida repeated the words slowly, letting the wonderful news sink in. 'We can stay at Hawthorne Cottage?'

'Yes! Berwooomph! You can stay and you'll be most welcome. I'll be off now. Make sure Lollipop gets up to no more mischief.'

The grim thought of having to move to Ditch, which had been hanging over Cressida for weeks, was suddenly lifted. It felt like the sun had burst through a heavy, grey winter sky, dazzling the world with bright colours.

'You're staying in Wissop which is the best news in the world!' Sophie shrieked in delight.

Cressie grinned. Things had certainly turned out much better than she could have ever imagined. There was just one thing to think about now … the next production for the Daisy Drama Club!

Did you know ...
... you really CAN put on
the Daisy Drama Club's
version of *A Christmas Carol!*

Just email
scripts@beetleheart.co.uk
and we'll send you all the info!
Love from the

daisy drama club

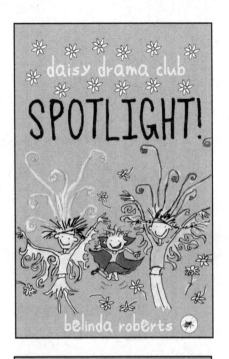

by belinda roberts

BOOKS

daisy drama club

www.daisydramaclub.co.uk

- Stage Fright! - Daisy Drama Club
- Spotlight! - Daisy Drama Club
- On Tour! - Daisy Drama Club

- Mr Darcy Goes Overboard
  (Sourcebooks)

PLAYS

- Angelica ... and the Monstrous, Monster of the Deep *
  (Samuel French)
  - Scrooge! *
  - Beetleheart *
  - Rose! ... and the Wicked Wolfee *
  - Christmas Candy *
  - Daydream Believer *
  - OTMA's Glory
  - Vivaldi's Angels
  - Starry Night
  - Pride, Pop and Prejudice
  - The Frog Princess
  - Trio : Creation • Jonah • The Real Mother

(* performed by the original Daisy Drama Club)

www.beetleheart.co.uk